Three Leaf Clover:
Aligned and Unaware

1

Three Leaf Clover: Aligned and Unaware

ERICA WIENER

This book is dedicated to my best friend, Scotty. Thank you for always believing in me, even when I didn't believe in myself. This book would not be possible without you. I love you.

PP

"In every single thing you do, you are choosing a direction. Your life is a product of choices."

Dr. Kathleen Hall

PART I
INTRODUCTION

ELIZABETH

Although the rain is coming down in sheets, nothing could put a damper on her mood. Since moving to the neighborhood a few weeks ago, Elizabeth has found not only a brand new lifestyle but also many new friends. As she finishes putting her hair into pink, hot curlers, her cell phone rings loudly in the next room. She gracefully walks the short distance from the master bathroom to the ringing in her bedroom.

It's her mother. Her heat sinks.

"Hi, dear. Sorry to bother you."

"No you aren't," Elizabeth clenched the phone harder.

Completely ignoring her daughter's rude comment, the woman continues. "Would you be interested in going to dinner with Patrick and me this evening?"

Elizabeth could feel her heart begin to pound. It starts slow at first, but continues to speed up as the silence increases. "Mom, stop."

"Elizabeth, sweetheart, we haven't seen you in awhile. We have so much to catch up on. I haven't told you the latest on..."

"Mom, we have nothing to catch up on," Elizabeth says. "I know you are aware I have plans for tonight. Brooke told me she ran into you yesterday. I know she told you about my dinner party."

An awkward silence follows. Connie is the first to break the silence.

"So, can we come?"

Elizabeth cannot stop herself from laughing. "Are you serious? Absolutely not! Remember what happened last time I invited you to my dinner party? You drank too much and pushed one of my friends off her chair." She pauses to take a breath. "I just made new friends! I have a new life now. I'm not even settled here and I won't let you ruin this for me. Before Elizabeth gives Connie a chance to respond, she shouts into the phone, "I want to be clear about this. You and Patrick are not welcome in my house. I'm serious about this. You cannot come."

"We would really like to see your new place. I don't even know where you moved to."

"Mom, that's the point. I needed a fresh start. Why can't you understand that?"

"I miss you."

Unable to find an ounce of sympathy or empathy, Elizabeth cuts her mother off again and throws her phone onto the bed. She paces back and forth trying to clear her head. The nerve of that woman! The way her mother treated Evan and herself growing up was nothing short of abusive. She was exposed to drugs and men at a young age. The longer she paces around, the more distraught she becomes. Not being able to calm down, she walks down the spiral staircase to the first level. Tears stream down her face. She brushes them away only to have another set take its place.

Her mind flashes back to her childhood once more. She spent half of her young years with her maternal grandparents. The feeling of abandonment engulfed everything she did. She hated spending time with her temperamental and sometimes irrational mother but she hated the feeling of not being around her. Although Elizabeth was and is very grateful for her grandparents, they were much too old to give her and her brother what they needed.

Elizabeth stops herself from dwelling any further on her past. She takes a deep breath and tries running her hands through her hair; temporarily forgetting about the curlers. Her fingers catch on several of them, pulling them out of place. She walks into the newly finished kitchen. The freshly installed marble countertops and the stainless steel appliances gleam as she turns on the light.

Still in a haze, she makes herself a cup of tea and leans against the counter. Realizing her grumpy mood is not subsiding, she picks up the phone and dials the number of her not much older brother.

After several rings, her brother finally answers.

"Hello?" he asks sleepily.

"Evan, are you seriously sleeping right now?"

"Yep," he mumbles. "Do you need something?"

"Yeah, Mom called."

Before Elizabeth could even continue, Evan groans through the phone. "Something tells me I know where this is going."

"Evan, listen, please. Mom wants to come to my dinner party. She really wants to bring Patrick, too."

"Of course she wants to come. She doesn't like that you don't talk to her. She's just looking for an excuse to catch up. She IS your mother, after all."

"Evan, I didn't call you so you can side with her."

"Well, you did call because you wanted some advice, right? Well, here it is. Mom is a very unreliable and irresponsible woman. I wouldn't trust her as far as I can throw her. In case you forgot, I broke my collar bone and can't lift anything." Elizabeth hears him snicker at his own joke. She begins to speak but Evan cuts her off. "Keeping what I said in mind, she is still your mother. She made many mistakes and I'm sure she's going to continue to do stupid things. However, I think you should give her a chance. Right or wrong, she's still your mother. You don't need to bend over backwards for her but if a situation brings itself to light, take advantage of it. If this helps, you're not inviting her to your dinner party. She's already invited herself over. You can be the better person and just allow her to come."

"But Patrick is going to be there, too. He hates me. I don't think I want someone like that in my house."

"Patrick doesn't hate you. He doesn't go out of his way to be nice to you because he knows you don't like him. When is the last time you gave him a chance?"

She thinks for a minute. Nothing comes to mind, however.

"I proved my point, didn't I?"

There is a short pause.

"Ok, Patrick-lover," she says. "I'm going to go. I still need to get ready for the party. I wish you could come."

"Yeah, me too. I'm proud of you though, sis."

Although Evan can't see her face, she smiles into the phone. "Thanks. I appreciate it."

"You're welcome. I'll see you later."

"Yeah, see ya later."

Elizabeth ends the call. Although the conversation with her brother was not particularly positive, listening to his logic always seems to calm her down. However, her mind is completely made up. Regardless of her mother's true intentions, Elizabeth knows she'll never be entirely comfortable with her mom and Patrick in her house.

She sits her cup down in the sink and heads back upstairs to get dressed. She slips into a short and tight black cocktail dress. She turns to look at herself in the full length mirror. Her reflection is nearly perfect. She turns around to look at the back of her legs. She takes a quick look to make sure the hem of her dress covers the small bruise. Even with her hair still in curlers, she's happy with her appearance. Trying to forget about her mother's phone call, she gently tugs the curlers out of her hair. Without much effort, the large, bouncy curls fall gracefully into place. She grabs the large bottle of hairspray and covers her head in a thick layer. As she slips on her shoes, she hears the front door open.

She walks out into the hallway and hollers down, "Hello?"

"Hi, honey!" The deep voice of her husband yells back. "Are you almost ready? They are going to be here soon."

"Yeah," she shouts.

She turns off the light in her bedroom and begins to walk downstairs. Standing in the foyer is Andrew in a freshly cleaned suit. He is holding a bouquet of pink and white roses.

Elizabeth tries to muster a sincere smile. "Are those for me?"

"They are," he says simply.

She takes them from him and turns back towards the kitchen to look for a vase. A strong grasp on her arm stops her in her tracks. She turns around to face Andrew. Elizabeth catches his gaze and drops her shoulders.

"Excuse me?"

Elizabeth allows her gaze to drop to the floor. "Thank you," she mumbles.

"You're welcome." Andrew releases her arm.

She turns back around and heads back into the kitchen. She hears Andrew climb the stairs and enter the bedroom. She digs through her cupboards, looking for her favorite glass vase. Coming up empty, she becomes slightly frantic.

"Andrew," she timidly says. Knowing Andrew isn't able to hear her, she decides to keep looking. She reenters the front room and begins digging through a tiny closet. She threw several pairs of shoes onto the floor. As she digs through the shelves, several boxes and a large bag come tumbling down onto the floor. The loud crash sends Andrew to the top of the stairs.

"Elizabeth? Are you ok?"

Being deep in her search, Elizabeth ignores him. She continues plowing through the shelves, emptying their contents onto the floor.

"What are you doing?"

The sound of alarm in his voice causes Elizabeth to stop what she's doing.

"Where is my blue vase from Grandma? The dark blue one with the white flowers on it."

"I don't know. Did you check in the cupboard by the stove?"

Elizabeth takes a deep breath, uncertain if she's sensing some annoyance in his voice.

"I did," she says quietly. "It's not there."

"I don't know, then."

She frantically continues her search in the closet. She can't stop the tears from welling up in her eyes. Unable to come up with the desired vase, panic sets in. She races up the stairs to check another closet. In her rush, she runs right into Andrew, bouncing off his chest. She almost knocks the vase out of his hand.

"Where did you find it?" She couldn't stop herself from shouting at him, automatically assuming he was hiding it from her.

"Calm down, it was in the hall closet. You must have put it in there after you used it last."

Unwilling to admit she may have over-reacted, she says, "Well, if I'd had it last, I would have put it back where it belongs."

Before another word can be said between either person, Elizabeth grabs her vase, turns on her heels and retreats back to the kitchen to put together her flower bouquet. Once completed, she looks at her arrangement, proud of herself. She gently places the flowers on the coffee table in the sitting room. After rearranging the flowers again, she smiles again. Perfect, she thinks to herself. She quickly cleans up her mess in the closet. Just as she shuts the door, the doorbell rings. She sprints to the closest bathroom. "Andrew! Can you get the door?" She quickly reapplies a layer of pale pink lipstick. She digs through a drawer and quickly locates the can of hair spray. She fluffs her hair as she hears another round of rings from the front door.

"Andrew, can you get the door, please? I'm almost ready."

When there is still no answer from Andrew, she quickly resprays her new, bouncy curls, checks her flawless make up, and pulls down the hem of her dress. She rushes to the door, her palms sweaty from anticipation. Standing in the doorway are two young couples. Brooke and Matt Brown, neighbors who live to the left of Elizabeth and Andrew, were the first people to welcome them to the neighborhood. Andrew also works with Matt. They are both cordial when they get together but they rarely speak to one another in the office.

"Hello, guys!" Elizabeth exclaims with a sincere smile on her face.

Brooke leans in and gives Elizabeth a kiss on the cheek. Elizabeth takes a step back. This type of greeting is common around their circle of friends but the custom is still new to Elizabeth. Unfortunately for her, Matt leans forward and gives Elizabeth a quick peck on the cheek, too.

"This house is very pretty!" Brooke says, taking a small step forward and looking around.

Andrew walks up and joins Elizabeth at the door. He quickly shakes hands with Matt.

Awkward silence follows. Finally Brooke speaks, breaking the silence. "Oh! I almost forgot. This is for you." She reaches around and grabs the extra-large tote from her shoulder. She pulls out a bottle of wine. "It's just a little house warming gift for you both."

Elizabeth gratefully takes the bottle from her. She gestures the two couples inside. Once she closes the door, the other couple steps forward. Elizabeth quickly hugs Tonya (relieved to not receive an awkward peck on the cheek) but is slightly hesitant with the much older man standing next to her.

Noticing the hesitation, Tonya says, "Oh, this is my boy-friend, Sean." She looks at her boyfriend and says, "Sean, this is Elizabeth and her husband ..."

Elizabeth doesn't skip a beat. "Andrew," she interjects.

Andrew claps his hands together. "Now that we're all acquainted, why don't we go to the sitting room?"

"Good idea," Elizabeth says.

Elizabeth and Andrew lead the way into the sitting room. The front doorbell rings again just as everyone is getting comfortable. Elizabeth excuses herself from the room. As she nears the front door, her husband meets her halfway.

"I'll get the door, go back to the guests."

Something in his voice causes Elizabeth to question him. She pauses. When he once again insists, she smiles thank-fully but hesitantly and returns to her guests. As she gets to the doorway of the sitting room, she hears the front door open and the booming voice of her husband echo back to her. She walks in and sits down in a chair across from Tonya and Sean. The five-some sip wine and resume their conversation.

"Hey honey, look who's here!"

Everyone looks up at the doorway. Elizabeth stares in horror, anger, and embarrassment. Her mother and stepfather stand next to Andrew. Her mother stood to the left, wearing a pair of bleached jeans with several holes in the knees. The neckline of her baby blue sweater dips dangerously low. Her curly, graying hair is slicked back into a bun, accentuating her large forehead. Patrick's attire is no better. His wrinkled, burgundy sweatshirt and tight, black jeans look as appalling as Connie's.

Elizabeth gets to her feet, nearly dropping her half-empty wine glass onto the carpet. Her heart pounds deep in her chest and she can feel her face flush. She looks over at Andrew with a combination of anger and disgust.

"Andrew, what's going on?"

"Hey sweetheart," Andrew says. "Why don't we let them get settled and you and I go talk in the kitchen."

"No," Elizabeth snaps. "I'd rather not."

"Actually, let's go talk." Andrew walks up to Elizabeth and gently but convincingly takes her arm. Reluctantly, she leaves the room but not before she glares at the extremely underdressed couple. Elizabeth summons all her strength to control her anger until they arrive in the kitchen. As the door closes behind him, Elizabeth turns and smacks her husband's arm a few times.

"Andrew! What is going on? Did you know about this?" she pauses. "You knew about this, didn't you? Please tell me you didn't."

"She called this afternoon. She wanted to surprise you. I thought you may get upset but I thought you haven't talked to her in a while. Thought it might be nice to see her."

"Oh, come on! You don't honestly believe I'd like to see…"

Andrew hushes her. Elizabeth, however, will not be quieted. "You know exactly how I feel about her. She called me earlier and tried to invite herself over. I told her no. Regardless, you shouldn't trust her in our house."

"Lizzy."

"Don't call me that." Elizabeth crosses her arms bitterly.

"Elizabeth, grow up a little bit and give this a chance. Let's go enjoy the party." He pauses to let the statement sink in.

She doesn't have a chance to respond before the doorbell rings again. Feeling helpless, she spats, "Just go answer the door."

Elizabeth storms out of the kitchen and rejoins the party. Her mother and stepfather have taken a seat across from the Browns. Elizabeth takes a seat back in her favorite chair. She leans forward and grabs her glass of wine. She quickly downs the contents of the glass as she listens to her mother tell

stories about as tall as her new ceilings. She bites her tongue
as she listens to her mother. Her anger slowly builds.

"Hi, Elizabeth!"

As she hears her name, Elizabeth instinctively gets to
her feet. Katharine and her husband, Josh, walk into the living room. Elizabeth gives her new friends a quick smile and
a hug and introduces them to the other guests. Once the
greetings are over, with Elizabeth leading the way, the group
head into the large dining room for dinner. Everyone takes a
seat at the long, oak table. The hired help bring out plates of
potatoes, pork, ham, roasted vegetables, freshly baked bread,
and lots and lots of wine.

Once the table is full of food and drinks, Elizabeth gets
to her feet. "I'd like to say a few things. First, I'd like to thank
everyone for coming. It really means a lot to Andrew and
me that all of you have come to celebrate our new house.
Secondly, I've been really nervous to move here because I
was so nervous to meet new people. But all of you have been
so supportive. You guys have made the move so much easier.
Thank you all." She raises her glass and everyone follows suit.

After the toast, Elizabeth sits down and smiles at her
husband across the table. He doesn't smile back. She slumps
a little bit in her seat at the lack of support.

"So are ya'll neighbors of Elizabeth?"

Once again, the sinking feeling in Elizabeth's stomach
returns at the sound of her mother's voice. Connie looks
around the table. The couples all hesitate to answer. Finally,
Tonya answers, "No, we're not all neighbors. You've raised a
very nice, young woman."

Connie beams.

"So, what do you do for a living?" Josh sips his drink
but looks expectantly at Connie. With no hesitation, Connie
states, "Oh, I'm not really working. I do odd jobs but for the
most part, I don't do anything. My husband handles most of

our finances." She leans over and pats Patrick on the arm. "I have a bad back, you know."

Without missing a moment, Patrick chimes in, "I work in customer service. I've been doing that for several years at different places so I'm pretty good. Actually, got employee of the month a couple months ago."

Awkward silence ensues again.

Unsure of what to do to break the silence, Elizabeth looks nervously at her husband. His head is down, looking at his phone.

Changing the subject, Brooke looks over at Katharine. "Did you tell Elizabeth what you are working on now? I think she'd like your latest project."

Elizabeth looks thankfully at Brooke for a second then her full attention jumps to Katharine. "Oh! What are you doing?"

Katharine sits up higher in her chair, no doubt proud of her latest accomplishment. "I'm throwing a benefit dinner in a few months. It's taking more time to orchestrate than I had originally thought but it's coming along quite well."

Elizabeth excitedly exclaims, "So, what kind of benefit is it? Is this something Andrew and I can contribute to?"

"Oh my! Of course you both are going to be invited. I'm working with a woman now on the invitations. Let me tell you a story first. It'll make more sense after I explain something."

Elizabeth leans in, preparing herself for what she has to say.

"Ok, so my cleaning lady's name is Martha. She has a young daughter, whom I forget her name now, Tracy, or something like that. Anyway, Martha didn't come right out and say it for about a year but she's had many issues with her daughter. She's very antisocial. She won't speak to anyone, including her parents. It's strange. She's very into math and does better than most in her class in that subject but cannot read for the absolute life of her. Finally, after talking to her about it, she came out and told me her daughter had been diagnosed with something called autism spectrum disorder. I researched it and I discovered that although it's more common than I had originally thought, there is not much information on a cause or a solution. So, I'm having a benefit dinner to help raise money for that research. I've talked Martha into bringing her daughter, too."

Elizabeth sits back in her chair, impressed her new friend can put something like that together. "That sounds amazing. If you need help with anything, let me know. Andrew and I would love to be a part of something like that."

Catching on quickly, Andrew jumps in. "Oh, absolutely. Let me know what we can do."

Josh puts his arm around his wife and gives her a quick peck on her temple. He looks very lovingly at her. "I'm very proud of her."

Seeing the love between husband and wife, Elizabeth can't help but think of her own relationship with her husband. They've been married only a short time but they've been together almost five years. They met on a blind date set up by her cousin. Elizabeth wasn't taken by Andrew at first. She always thought he was good looking but being more on the shy side, she was too nervous to approach him. A few months later, though, they began dating. They've been together ever since. After the birth of their twins, however, Andrew began working more and more. He leaves early in the morning and doesn't come home until after dinner time. It can be very lonely.

Elizabeth can't stop herself from feeling jealous. She looks over at Andrew. He has his head down and is staring at his cell phone again. After a brief moment, he looks up at her. He flashes a quick smile. She fills with disappointment as she realizes she no longer gets butterflies in her stomach when he smiles at her. She wonders when that all changed.

"Elizabeth?"

Elizabeth snaps back to reality. Everyone at the table is looking at her. "Oh! Sorry, I was in my own world. What did I miss?"

"Your mother is telling us about the trips you guys took when you were younger. I asked you which one you liked best."

Elizabeth instantly becomes upset. Her mother had taken Evan and herself on exactly two trips. The first one was when she was very little. She'd gotten lost at a large park. A nice couple found her crying and alone. They took her to a small security station. The people in charge made several announcements over the loud speaker. Unfortunately, no one came forward to claim her. After a few hours, a police officer came to pick her up. Elizabeth remembers crying the entire time. She spent the night in the police station, sleeping in a dark room by herself on a cot made for a small house cat. Her second experience wasn't any better. Although she'd been older, the experience was just as traumatizing. Connie and her boyfriend at the time, Paul, had taken the children to a small cottage in the middle of the woods. It had rained all day and all the night before. Everyone had grown restless. Paul went out for a walk outside. He never came back. He was found two miles away from the cottage with a bullet in his head.

"Mom, let's not go there," Elizabeth said. "You and I both know how our trips turned out and I don't feel like it's appropriate party conversation."

Connie isn't deterred by her daughter's outrage. "My favorite time was when we took you kids up to the mountains." She makes sure to face the company as she speaks. "It was really cold outside but your grandparents loved spending the extra time with you both."

Elizabeth contemplates jumping in and contradicting her but decides to ignore her mother's lies.

Connie continues, "Do you remember the last time we were there? I know it was quite some time ago."

"Mom, you never took us to the mountains. Evan and I begged you to let us go, but you wouldn't." She begins to raise her voice. "What is your deal? What's the point in making this big, elaborate lie anyway? No one here cares."

"Elizabeth! I didn't raise you to talk to me like this! What has gotten into you?"

"That's just it, Mom, you didn't raise me. You spent more time with your boyfriends or husbands, than taking care of us."

Andrew, unsure of how to diffuse the situation, lays his head onto his hands. "Elizabeth, honey, would you like more wine?"

"Sure, sweetheart," she says sarcastically. "Maybe if I drink more, I may actually appreciate my mother's company." Nobody passes Elizabeth the freshly opened bottle of wine but she gladly gets to her feet and grabs it herself. "Anybody want more? If not, I'm probably going to drink the whole thing."

No one answers. The rest of the dinner is eaten in silence. Although the food tastes good, nobody asks for seconds. Nobody asks for another glass of wine. Once the dinner is over, they all stand up. Everyone follows Andrew into the sitting room, except for Elizabeth who stays behind. She watches them walk away. Once her guests are out of sight, she sighs deeply and rolls her eyes. What an awful night. She leaves the table and walks into the kitchen. Sitting on the counters are trays of cookies, cakes, and assortment of chocolates. She carries the tray of goodies into the living room where everyone is waiting quietly. She plasters a smile on her face, even though the anger is close to boiling over.

Everyone is sitting down with the exception of Connie and Patrick. They, instead, are standing by the door. Elizabeth doesn't get the opportunity to say anything before Connie speaks.

"Me and Patrick are going to head out. We weren't planning on staying very long. This was a nice party and your friends are lovely. Thanks for inviting us."

Elizabeth takes a deep breath then mumbles, "Thanks." Elizabeth cannot muster up even a half smile to give to her mother. She watches as her mother begins to walk over to her with her arms outstretched. She takes a step back but Connie doesn't take the hint. She continues walking toward Elizabeth and embraces her. Elizabeth doesn't hug back. When Connie steps back, Elizabeth doesn't make eye contact with her. "Ok, well, we're going to go then. It was nice meeting everyone." Connie smiles at the other guests.

"It was nice to meet you, too," Josh says. Several others nod in agreement.

"Would you like me to walk you to the door?" Andrew asks.

"Uhhh … no that's ok, we'll find our way out. Thanks." Connie adds, "Thanks for inviting us."

"Yeah, thanks guys," Patrick agrees.

Without another word, the awkward couple turns around and leaves the room. Nobody says a word. They listen to the sound of the front door both open and close. Elizabeth breathes a sigh of relief. She tries to enjoy her party but the overwhelming feeling of sadness, loss, and anger makes it nearly an impossible feat.

GEORGE

Light trickles into the tiny bedroom. George slowly opens his eyes. He allows himself several moments to let his eyes adjust to the morning. He sits up and stretches his arms over his head. He turns around, looking at the lump in the bed to his left. He smiles. He leans over, withdrawing the blanket from around her face. He tenderly reaches over and brushes away a small piece of graying hair that has fallen in front of her closed eyes. She doesn't stir. He slides out of bed, his unforgiving bones preventing him from doing it quietly, however. He gently puts on his house shoes and shuffles into the small kitchen. As if it is second nature, he walks over to the refrigerator, gives the already wobbly handle a hard yank. It takes several tries but the door finally swings open. He pulls out the orange juice, shuts the door, and rummages through the cupboard trying to locate two tall, glass cups. He fills the cups but chooses to leave the now half-full carton of juice on the counter. He slowly walks out the front door and sees the two rocking chairs waiting for him. He plops down in his usual one and gently sets one glass of juice down onto the wooden porch floor.

"Morning, Mr. Perkowski!"

George's head snaps up and he looks around for the face that matches the voice. He locates the teenage paperboy. He waves back. "Good morning, Bryan."

He sits back in his chair and watches the neighborhood wake up. After fifteen minutes or so, a short, medium build, woman gently shuffles out and sits down in the adjoining rocking chair.

"Hi, sweetheart," she says softly.

With no hesitation, George smiles back lovingly. "Hi, beautiful." He reaches down and picks up the extra glass of orange juice. With shaking hands, he slowly hands it off to his wife. He sits back and continues to take in the sights of the amazing town. After some time has passed, George breaks the silence. "So, what is on the agenda today?"

Ever so quietly, Ethel responds. "My daughter is coming into town today. I told you about it last week, honey, remember?"

A sinking feeling comes over George but he tries not to show it. "I remembered; sort of. How long is she staying?"

"I don't know, dear."

"Ethel, honey..."

"Please don't start. If the topic comes up, I'll ask her about the loan. If not, I'm not going to push it. You know, she's going through a rough time right now. She just lost her job."

George tries to hide how angry he is. He opens his mouth to continue to argue but then shuts it. It's not worth it. He sits back in his chair and looks out into the street. There isn't much to look at during this time of the morning. Everything is quiet and calm. Finally, George speaks again. "I'm submitting my paperwork for work today." He sits up a little straighter in his chair, proud of the accomplishment.

"When will the paperwork go through?"

"I'm not sure when my retirement officially starts because that lady is on vacation but I told them about our planned vacation." He smiles both excitedly and lovingly.

His wife smiles back.

George glances down at his watch on his wrist and stretches for a few seconds. "I should probably get ready for work. It's a shame my retirement doesn't start now."

"Yeah," Ethel says quietly.

"I love you."

He gets to his feet and shuffles back into the house. He gently lays his glass down onto the kitchen counter and quickly returns to his bedroom. He changes into jeans, a clean white shirt, and his brown dress shoes. Although he doesn't have much hair left, he brushes it for a moment before heading back outside. Ethel's eyes are closed but she's quietly humming to herself and rocking back and forth in her chair.

"Bye, sweetie," he leans in and gently whispers into her ear.

"I love you."

"I love you. See you tonight."

George unsteadily walks off his already wobbly wooden steps. Although the walk to his car isn't long, his arthritic bones make the trip much longer. With shaking hands, he opens the car and finds himself struggling to climb into his luxuriously, large car.

"Humph," he says, once he finally manages it. He takes a deep breath before reaching over and shutting the car door. He doesn't look over to see if his wife is looking. She probably is. He spent countless hours trying to convince both Ethel and himself that his muscle aches are only minor and temporary. It isn't working. He slowly backs the car out of the driveway, mindful of all the other drivers. As he makes the short drive to the post office, he tries to remain positive. The last time his stepdaughter came to town, she borrowed a large sum of money and has yet to pay it back; or even make a small payment. The money isn't the issue. It's the constant promises to pay and the excuses that follow that upset him.

He sighs. Ethel can be very blinded by her family.

Honk, honk.

The sound distracts him from his thoughts. He looks in his rearview mirror, not sure what he expects to see. When nothing seems out of the ordinary, he focuses back on the road in front of him. He is just about to let his mind wander back to his own family when the honking resumes.

He glances in his mirror again and sees several cars driving close behind him. He takes his eyes off the tiny mirror and puts them to his speedometer; noticing he's only slightly under the speed limit. He sits back, now ignoring the multiple honks that follow along with him for the short drive. When he gets close to work, he drives even slower. No point in spending more time in that unorganized, mismanaged, loud and busy back office.

Honk.

George doesn't have to look behind him this time. He already knows what the scene looks like. He slows down to a near stop and turns on his right turn signal. After pausing for a moment, he slowly turns his boat of a car into the already busy parking lot.

"Hey, George!"

George barely has time to climb out from his usual parking spot before someone is calling his name. He looks around for the source of the noise. He locks eyes with his direct supervisor, Scott. Scott breaks the eye contact and his eyes fall directly onto his watch. Although George knows he is more than half an hour early as usual, he braces himself for a confrontation.

"Oh. I thought we discussed you coming in early this week since half the front line is on vacation."

"We did. I am here early."

"George, a few minutes doesn't help anyone. Please go clock in."

Trying to remain calm, George chooses instead to think about his upcoming beach vacation. He staggers into the post office and quickly locates the time clock. He punches in, making sure to keep his head down so as not to draw any more attention to himself. He goes about his business, cleaning up spills and messes, de-cluttering his work station, passing packages out to the correct department, and not talking to anyone. After more than six hours of the same routine, without an interruption, he clocks out. He rummages through his deep pockets, trying to locate his keys. Struggling to steady his shaking hands, he rips the keys out of his right pocket, along with pieces of thread. He unsteadily walks out of the building, grateful to see the sunshine again. The parking lot is not even half full of cars; most of which are probably not employees. As he nears his car, he turns around and looks at the post office.

"Good riddance!"

It's only a matter of time before he gets to walk out and never return. The thought does calm his agitated nerves. He climbs back into his car and without much thought, drives back to his house. As he pulls into the driveway, any remaining happiness inside of him plummets to his toes, along with his stomach. There is an extra car in the driveway. Although he doesn't recognize the car, he has a disappointing idea who the owner is. He sighs deeply. He tries to find any remaining energy he has and he uses it to plaster on the biggest, fakest smile he can muster. As he emerges out of his car, he even practices a few fake laughs to make sure it sounds sincere.

Check.

"Hi, dear."

He doesn't have to open the door. Ethel stands at the front door with a similarly placed smile. George struggles to maintain his happy demeanor.

"Hi, honey," Ethel says in response.

George detects her usual shy and nervous tone. The tone she only uses when she is hiding something. George doesn't step into the house. He stands in front of Ethel, awaiting more of an explanation. When she doesn't offer one, George places his hands on his hips.

"She's in there, isn't she?"

He watches Ethel's eyes as they leave his gaze and fall to the porch floor. "Who, sweetie?"

"Bethany."

With her eyes still diverted to her feet, she mumbles, "Yes."

Angry but not at all surprised, George sighs again.

"Ok." He pauses, trying to pick his words carefully. "Let's go inside so I can say 'hello.'"

George notices the look of surprise on Ethel's face but decides not to offer his own explanation for the friendlier response. Ethel turns around and holds the door open so George can enter. What he sees next takes his breath away. Not one, not two, not three, but four children are running around between the living room, dining room, and narrow hallway. The volume level in the house has more than quadrupled. Among the chaos sits a woman with dark blonde hair which is perfectly styled, well-manicured nails, expertly applied make-up, and wearing name brand clothes. George fights his first impulse to turn around and leave.

"Hi, Bethany! He says, trying not to sound overly enthusiastic or fake. "Got a bunch of kids now, huh?"

Bethany smiles. "They aren't all mine, Pops. This one (she points at the back of the head of a blonde boy) aaannndddd ..." she pauses while she searches for the correct kid among the mess. "This one!" she finally shouts when she locates the red headed monster, "are Jamie's two kids. You already know my two already."

"Jamie? Is that the new boyfriend? What does this one do? He's not an artist like Benji was, is he?"

"Jamie is a woman, Pops."

"A what?"

"You heard me."

Flabbergasted, George sputters, "W-w-when did this happen? Did you know about this?" George throws a confused look at his wife.

"Not until today," is all she says in response.

No adults speak for the next minute and a half. George and Ethel stare at Bethany in awe while Bethany switches her glance back and forth between her parents with a smirk on her face. The children continue to run around them. A loud crash breaks the awkward silence.

"Max! Anna! Benjamin! Eli! Who broke what?!"

For the first time since George stepped into the house, the house is dead silent. It is eerie. George waits to hear a pin drop.

"Max! Anna! Benj…" A timid little head pokes around the corner, which stops Bethany's rant. "Annabelle Marie, what did you do?"

"Nothing."

Although Anna is across the room from her, Bethany makes it in front of her in microseconds. "I asked you a question that requires an answer." She reaches out and grabs the little girl's arm. The motion startles George. He's never put his hands on any of his kids and he never imagined any of his kids would respond this way. George watches as Bethany squeezes her arm. It quickly goes from a healthy peach color to a red and quickly to a white. "I'm going to ask you again. I heard glass breaking. What did you do?"

Anna looks frightfully at George. In that instant, George forgets about the anger and frustration building inside of him. He smiles and walks over to them. He gently places his hand on Bethany's arm. She instantly lets go of the child's arm. He gently rubs the marks on the little gir's arm to get the circulation going again.

He kneels down in front of her and with his most genuine smile, says, "I think I heard some glass break. Are you ok?"

Anna doesn't immediately respond. When there is no more yelling, Anna sheepishly returns the smile. "Yeah," she mumbles.

"Well that's good!" George says happily. "Do you think we should go clean it up before your crazy brothers step in it?"

"Yeah."

Although Anna's answer is quiet, George notices a slight grin.

"Alright, can you get all your brothers into the living room for me while I get a broom, a dust pan, and a trash can?"

"Uh-huh." The little girl scampers away.

George gives Bethany a sideways glance. She doesn't say anything in response. He rolls his eyes as he walks away to help with the mess in the back bedroom.

As he walks in, he can't stop himself from feeling sad when he sees the broken picture frame. He kneels down next to it to assess the damage. Thankfully, the photograph inside seems to be fine. He picks it up and shakes off as much of the shattered glass as he can. Anna walks in. As soon as she sees George looking at her mess, she stops dead in her tracks. She hesitantly looks up at George with frightened eyes, awaiting another round of yelling.

"Is this what happened?"

The child nods.

"Ok. Well, very carefully, come here." He outstretches his hand to the girl. She takes several uncertain steps toward George. When she gets close to him, she takes his hand. He helps lead her toward him but away from the large shards of glass. He grabs the trash can. "Alright, Anna, dear. Can you hold this for me?"

She gives another small, uncertain smile and nods her head. After a few short minutes, all of the glass is picked up and thrown into the small trash can. Just as the last piece is chucked into the plastic can, two of the boys come bolting into the room.

"Anna! Come play!" the oldest boy shouts.

Anna looks hopefully at George. George smiles back at her and says, 'Go ahead. Thanks for your help with the glass." Anna skips away and George finishes picking up the broken wood frame.

When George is finished, he reenters the living room. All is quiet. The silence shocks him. When he recovers, he finds Ethel sitting in one of the two armchairs.

"Where is everyone?"

An exhausted Ethel looks up. "They are going to the park."

"Are they coming back?"

"They are."

George sighs. He goes to the kitchen and gets a glass of water. He fills it ¾ full and carefully takes it to his exhausted wife.

"Thank you."

George sits down in the adjacent chair. Although he tries to stop it from occurring, his eyes become too heavy and they finally close.

CAMERON

The alarm buzzing loudly on the bedside table abruptly brings the sleeping couple back to consciousness.

"Ughhh…"

"Honey, the alarm … off …" she mumbled sleepily.

Cameron groans again but this time he rolls toward the increasingly, obnoxious black box. After smacking the alarm clock a few times, both the buzzing and the high-pitched ringing come to a sudden halt. The room becomes oddly quiet.

Scratch, scratch.

Cameron squeezes his eyes shut and very quietly mumbles, "Go away, go away, please, go away."

"Cam, he's not going to go away."

Cameron contemplates trying to ignore the scratching on the bedroom door but his decision is quickly made for him when an elbow jabs him in his already tender ribs.

"Alright, I'm up," he angrily mumbles as he rolls out of bed. He stumbles to the door. No sooner did the door open, a large, 75 lb, black lab mix pounces onto the bed. The mass already situated in the bed, barely moves as the dog curls up in the now vacant spot. Rolling his still sleepy eyes, Cameron exits their bedroom and walks the short distance down the narrow hallway to the kitchen. Without much thought, he drags himself to the large coffeepot. Very robotically, he fills the pot with strong coffee. When he finishes, he walks slowly back through the hallway, careful not to wake his sleeping son. He runs his hand along the smooth, pale, green walls. He reenters the master bedroom. He glances at the bed, which is still being occupied by his wife and dog. Claire's arm is lazily thrown across a furry neck. Both breathing bodies are snoring loudly. Cam cannot stop himself from smiling as he opens the sliding oak door that leads to the master bathroom.

He quietly steps inside and completely slides the door shut before slipping on the bright light and turning on the shower.

He strips off his pajamas and after checking the temperature of the running water, hops into the shower. He allows the cool water to wash over him. He fights the urge to let his mind wander to the recent events. His heart begins to race. Why did I open her email? Cameron thinks sadly. I should have minded my own business.

"No," he says aloud when the short email flashes in front of him. He squeezes his eyes shut tight, willing the flashes to go away. Unfortunately, he fails as his mind takes over and replays the life altering cyber-note.

Sweetheart,

Thank you for sending me those pictures of CJ and Charli. I still can't believe how big he has gotten. My plane is still expected to arrive around 3:30. I can't wait to see you.

With love,
Lee

With the usual negative emotions building up inside, Cameron can feel his eyes beginning to fill with tears. No, he tells himself. He turns around and turns the water entirely on hot. The scalding water begins to burn his already tan back. He flinches but neither turns the water onto cool nor turns it off. The intense heat does one thing his brain could not; it clears his mind of all his thoughts. All his anxieties, his worries, and his pain swirl around the drain of the shower and disappear.

After fifteen minutes of the mind-numbing shower, he reluctantly turns off the water. He steps out of the shower. He slips on the water on the floor and comes tumbling down onto the tiled floor. He lands on all fours, pain shooting into his knees.

"Ow!" he loudly moans before getting back to his feet. He wraps a towel around himself. He quietly opens the bathroom door, expecting to see his wife still sleeping in the bed. However, as the light from the bathroom illuminates the bedroom, he can see his bed is empty.

He walks to the open bedroom door and closes it. He changes into his usual work attire. Leaving his suit jacket unbuttoned, he walks out into the hallway and back into the kitchen. His wife is sitting at the table quietly drinking a steaming mug of black coffee.

"Good morning," she quietly mumbles.

"Good morning," he answers her in a similar tone of voice. "Sleep alright?"

There's a slight pause. "Yeah, thanks."

Unsure of what else to say, Cam walks over to the coffee pot and pours himself a large cup. "I have a long day planned today. I'm not sure when I'm going to be home tonight."

Claire never looks up from her cup. "Ok. I don't have any other plans than to see Mom. I guess I'll be here to get CJ."

Cam detects a hint of anger in her voice. He chooses to ignore the tone. "Is CJ still sleeping?"

Claire finally glances up at Cam. He's surprised to see the look on her face. "Cam, stop trying to make small talk. Of course he's still sleeping. He doesn't get up for at least another forty-five minutes. You know that," she adds shortly.

"Claire, come on. Do you want to talk about anything?"

Claire stands up and walks over to the sink. Cam watches her drop her coffee mug into the sink next to a few dirty dishes from the night before. She purposely makes a large circle around Cameron to avoid getting too close to him. She mumbles, "No."

Cam reaches out and attempts to grab Claire's arm. He misses. He watches her walk out of the room and into the small sitting room. He glances at the clock by the stove. Realizing he has much more time on his hands before he needs to leave for work, he quickly drinks the rest of his piping hot coffee. Walking back to the coffeepot, he pours himself another cup and sits down in Claire's seat. He thinks about looking at his monthly sports magazine but opts to stare into the hallway; letting his mind wander again over his very long list of to do's. He thinks of all the patients he needs to see, all the paperwork that needs completed, the long conference in the afternoon that he needs to attend, and all the long phone calls that he needs to make.

As Cam continues to stare into the hallway, a small shadow emerges. Cam snaps back to reality. A young boy stumbles sleepily into the sitting room. Cam gets to his feet. Wanting to acknowledge his sleepy son, he walks into the sitting room as well. Claire is sitting on the couch working on yet another crossword puzzle. She looks up as Cam enters the room. She gives him a small, half smile. He takes his eyes off her and his eyes find CJ. He watches him sit down on the floor in front of his mother. He is holding his favorite book. CJ's large glasses struggle to stay in place as he feverishly searches through his book.

"Good morning, buddy."

CJ doesn't respond to his father's voice Cam isn't deterred by this lack of acknowledgement. "Whatcha looking at in your book? Can I see?"

CJ still continues to ignore Cam. Cam walks over to the boy and sits down on the floor. Not surprisingly, CJ is look-ing at the same book he's been obsessing over for a few weeks now. Pictures of spaceships and the solar system stare back at them. Although Cam is used to being ignored by his son, it still hurts. He smiles at the boy and rubs his back for a short time. Then he looks up at his wife. Claire's head is down as she scrutinizes over the puzzle.

"I love you," he says somewhat quietly.

She doesn't respond. Although she doesn't lift her head up, she does briefly stop working on her puzzle. Cam looks back down at the floor. He runs his hand over the carpet.

"Ow!"

Sharp pain shoots into his left hand. He pulls out yet another nail nestled deep in the carpet.

"Is that another nail? I thought you cleaned up in here."

Cam looks down at his hand, thankful the small nail barely broke the skin. He looks back at his wife. "I thought I did get everything," he snapped. "Clearly I missed one."

"Clearly. Did you actually vacuum the floor?"

Not wanting to fight in front of CJ but knowing an argument is not far away, he says, "No, I did not, sweetheart. I'm going to head to work now. This may be a long day. I'll call you later."

He gives his son a quick kiss on the top of his head and climbs to his feet. He gets to the doorway when Claire's voice stops him.

"Did you forget something?"

He gives his wife a smile and walks over to her. He leans toward her to kiss her good-bye. She quickly pulls away before he can make contact with her. He stands back up looking quizzically at Claire.

"You left the nail on the floor."

Angrily, Cam grabs the nail and leaves the room. He enters the kitchen again and throws the nail into the trash can under the sink. Grabbing his bag and coat, he leaves the house through the side door.

He walks outside toward the car. Along the way, he passes a large cardboard box containing old newspapers. Balling up his fist, he punches the box twice to try to relieve his frustration. When it fails to make him feel better, he gives the brick wall a punch. Pain explodes from his hand and radiates up his arm. He glances down and blood begins to pour out of his battered hand. He quickly grabs a towel from his car and wraps his hand.

With his throbbing hand, he drives the half an hour to the hospital. He pulls into the physicians' parking lot. When he gets out of the car, he takes a quick glance at his watch. He still has about forty minutes before his first appointment so he heads straight to his office. As he quickly walks to the other side of the hospital, he hears a familiar voice exclaim, "Good morning, Dr. Johnson." Cam ignores the voice. He continues on his trek toward his office. He unlocks the door and before anyone can approach him, he shuts it. He unwraps his hand and looks at the damage he caused.

Knock, knock, knock.

Cam looks up at the door. Before he can say anything, the door opens. Standing in the doorway, is a petite, young woman. She is staring at Cam's exposed hand.

"Rough morning, huh?"

Unsure of exactly what to say, he mumbles, "Yeah, rough morning."

The young nurse smiles understandingly and disappears from the doorway. He turns away from the door and begins to look for something to fix his bloody hand. His undamaged hand falls onto his favorite picture. The black, wooden frame holds one of the few smiling pictures of CJ. In the background are several spotted cows and a chicken. That day was perfect. The sky was cloudy but the temperature was warm. CJ was interactive and happy. Seeing the look of astonishment, wonder, and curiosity on his son's face made the trip well worth the long drive. Although the trip to the farm was over a year ago, it was the last father and son outing.

Cam smiles at the picture even though the feeling of sadness begins to creep back up.

He hears another knock at the door. He quickly hides his hand. The young woman opens the door and walks in holding several towels and bandages.

"Let me help you."

"Jen, you don't have…"

"I know I don't have to."

Jennifer quickly cleans up Cam's broken hand. Cam looks into Jennifer's soft brown eyes. Realizing his heart skips a beat, he looks away. He thanks her and heads out of the office, leaving her standing by herself. He hurriedly walks to the other side of the hospital, noticing for the first time he's about to be late to his first appointment. Feeling obligated to speak to only two people during his brisk walk, he makes it to his destination a few minutes late. He stands outside of the door, trying to ready himself.

This year marks the tenth anniversary Cam has been working for the hospital. It has never gotten easier. Not only is the hospital extremely understaffed but the minimal people they do have are undereducated. The one thing the hospital does not lack, however, are patients. With such a small group of employees, the level of stress is overwhelming most days. During a usual day, Cam runs around from room to room, doing his absolute best to equally serve all of his patients. However, at the end of every day, he feels as though nothing is ever accomplished. Taking a deep breath, he walks into his first appointment, determined this one will be different.

JULIA

Julia climbs the five, small, wooden steps to the front door of her apartment complex. She quickly opens the rickety front door and ducks inside. Water pours off her and puddles at her feet. She turns around to look outside but she can't see a thing. The darkness has begun to settle. Turning away from the dreary sight outside, Julia focuses on the dreary sight inside.

Unfortunately, the stairwell leading to the second floor is on the opposite end of the complex. Rearranging her navy blue book bag on her shoulder, she makes the trek toward the stairwell. Every day, around this time, it's the same thing. The person who is living in the first room on the left is a bit of a hermit. No one in Julia's family, Julia included, has ever laid eyes on anyone entering or leaving the apartment. The only sound is the loud voice of a news anchor discussing the current events or occasionally a deep, raspy cough.

Crash.

Julia jumps back. The sound comes from across the hall. She puts her back against the filthy wall. She looks at the apartment door, half-expecting it to open. It does not. Another loud crash interrupts her thoughts. Although a loud racket is a regular occurrence in the complex, it is still startling. She continues down the hallway. From somewhere behind her, she hears a door open. She, however, doesn't turn around.

"Hey!" a male voice shouts.

Panic-stricken, Julia starts running. She runs as fast as she can to the stairwell. She flings open the door and takes the gray, cement stairs two at a time. Throwing open the door to the second level, she leaps onto the carpeted floor. The upper level is significantly quieter than the lower level. She contemplates turning around to see if anyone is following her. Deciding not to chance it, she runs to her own apartment. She fumbles for a second with the keys then quickly unlocks the door. She opens the door to her apartment, thankful for once to be in a safe place. She shuts the door behind her, closing it harder than she intends. Although the apartment is dark and cold, Julia knows she's not alone.

"Hello?"

No answer.

"Allen, come on. You know I hate when you do this. I hear you breathing."

A voice of a drunken, young man answers through the darkness. "Well, stop being stupid."

Although Allen can't see her through the darkness, Julia rolls her eyes anyway. She pulls her bleached blonde hair into a messy ponytail. She walks to the far side of the room and turns the light on. Once her eyes adjust to the brightness, her eyes settle on a tall, dark, and handsome man sitting on the couch; beer in one hand, cell phone in the other.

"You bring me food?"

Julia angrily responds, "No! I've been in class all day."

Allen staggers to his feet. "What's that supposed to mean? You think you're better than me?"

He takes a step toward Julia, shoving her down to the floor. On her way down, she lands on top of an orange and white tabby cat. The cat screeches and scampers away. From prior experience, Julia knows not to get to her feet until Allen allows her. Several tense seconds go by before either speaks.

"I want your mom's keys. I gotta go."

Julia continues to sit on the floor, unsure of what to do.

Allen kneels onto the floor next to her. He grabs her arm, squeezing it tightly.

"Mom ... keys ... now."

Julia hurriedly gets to her feet. Her heart is pounding. "Yeah, sure. Gimme a second to find them."

Allen lets go of Julia's arm. She leaves the living room and very quietly enters her mother's bedroom. The room is dark and only the light from the television illuminates her sleeping mother. Julia steps forward and stands over her. Unsure of where the keys are, Julia begins to rummage through her mother's pockets. After coming up with nothing but nickels and pennies, Julia heads toward the wooden dresser next to the bed. Unable to see more than a few inches in front of her, she falls into something large, knocking many of its contents onto the carpet. After pausing to let her eyes adjust, she realizes she fell into the dresser. Even after the loud crash, her mother doesn't stir in the bed. The light in the bedroom clicks on. Julia spins around to face the doorway. Allen stands there with his hand on the light switch and an unhappy look on his face.

"Allen! What are you doing?" She loudly whispers.

"Your mom is wasted. She's not going to wake up. Look at her!"

Julia glances at her mother. Jossa's light brown hair is disheveled and covers her closed eyes. There is a noticeably large wet spot on the dark blanket.

"This is unbelievable," Julia groans. She walks back over to her mother and turns her over onto her side. She brushes the hair out of Jossa's eyes. Grabbing the small, half-empty vodka bottle out of her mother's hand, she rearranges the cream and pink colored blanket over her mother. Julia can't stop herself from shaking her head with both annoyance and disgust.

Her mother never moves a muscle.

"This is ridiculous. Jul, just get out of the way."

Allen roughly shoves past Julia and walks over to the dresser. Sitting amongst the beer bottles and paper plates is a key ring. There are only two keys on the key rings; one being the apartment key and the other being the much desired car key. Julia isn't sure if she should be happy, relieved, or disappointed he found the keys so quickly. Allen grabs the keys and before he stomps out of the bedroom, he makes a point to purposely and painfully run into her shoulder with his own. Slightly taken aback, Julia stands in the middle of the bedroom, looking at the mess on the floor. Clothes cover almost every inch of the floor. Placed at the foot of the bed and near the dresser were cases of empty, glass beer bottles. With nothing else planned for the night, she begins cleaning her mother's room while her mother lays passed out on the bed.

Half an hour later, Julia turns the light back off in Jossa's room. She walks back into the cramped living room. It is oddly quiet, not only in the apartment, but in the neighboring apartments, Julia realizes. Throwing herself onto the couch, she grabs the remote control. She flips through only a few channels before there is a loud knock at the door. Julia contemplates whether or not to ignore the knocking. Past experiences tell her that opening the door to an unknown person is not the best idea.

Her mind flashes back to three months ago. In the middle of eating dinner with her mother and young niece, there was a loud knocking at the door. Jossa tells her youngest daughter to answer the door. Julia remembers feeling uneasy but very reluctantly sets down her fork and gets to her feet. She walked toward the door. She turned around to look at her mother; secretly hoping Jossa would change her mind and let her ignore the knocking, she did not.

She very slowly unlocked the front door. She didn't have to open it, however, because the door flies open. Julia stumbled back as two men rushed in. One of the men grabbed Julia's arm while the other one makes a grab for Jossa. Julia heard her niece scream from the back of the room. Julia remembers instantly panicking. She tried to spin around to look at her niece but is unsuccessful. A firm hand keeps her in place.

"Gen!" she remembers screaming.

Julia snaps back to reality. Reminiscing about the break-in makes up Julia's mind. With the remote in her hand, she increases the volume on the television, ignoring the knocks. Eventually, the knocking ends. A wave of relief washes over her. She lowers the volume to a respectable level and settles down into the couch. Although it's only a little bit later than dinner time, Julia catches herself yawning every few minutes. Between watching her niece, going to school, and working her new job at the local deli, Julia barely has enough energy to finish the day. A short time later, her eyes close, and she drifts off to sleep.

She is walking through a dark hallway. Although there is no lamp or sunlight, her eyes have slightly adjusted to the darkness. Lockers line both sides of the hallway. It appears to be a high school but it isn't the high school she attends. Suddenly, a dark greenish-yellow mist rises from the floor. Julia realizes she cannot breathe. She coughs hard and starts running down the hall. If she can only get to the end of the hallway, maybe she can get out of here, she wishfully thinks. As the mist rises, she forces herself to run faster. The hallway seems to never end and it is becoming increasingly harder and harder to breathe. Her eyes begin to burn. Panicking, she sprints. Finally, she runs into something hard. It knocks her down. When she gets to her feet, she notices all the mirrors. The mist fades and her reflection stares back at her. She looks into her own eyes and sees nothing but fear. Her once flawless make-up is smudged and running down her face. Her cheeks are bright red from running. The collar of her t-shirt is torn. She tries to run her hands through her hair but it is nothing more than a tangled mess. She stares intently at herself. Why do I look like this? What is going on? Why is there a mirror? A

*million questions race through her mind; none of which she has
any answers for.*

Bang, bang, bang.

*She jumps back, looking around to find the cause. A door on
the opposite end of the hall slowly creaks open. Julia contemplates
whether or not to investigate. Deciding against it, she backs up as
far as possible from the opened door. She sinks to the floor, pulling
her knees close to her chest. Although she sees no one, she can hear
footsteps coming closer and closer. She puts her hands over her ears
and screams. "Leave me alone!"*

*She hears footsteps running toward her. She panics and
throws her hands over her head. She screams as two tiny hands
begin to shake her.*

She opens her eyes and a pair of eyes, matching in color
to her own, stare back at her. Julia quickly and instinctively
smiles, although her heart is racing. She reaches out and
grabs the little girl. The small child squeals with joy and
falls into her aunt's lap. After a minute of tickling, Julia stops
and sits up, trying desperately to catch her breath and gather
her bearings.

"Hey Gen, where's Mom?"

The four year old shrugs her shoulders. "I don't know.
She says I'm 'posed to stay here with you for awhile. Wanna
play a game?"

Julia glances at the clock. 11:42. "Actually, it is way past
your bedtime, don't you think? Let's go get milk, calm down,
and get ready for bed."

Although slightly disappointed, the girl gets to her
feet and scurries into the kitchen. Julia does the same and
slowly drags herself to the kitchen. She is still significantly
dazed from her dream. She slides her feet lazily on the wood
floor, knowing a long night lies in front of her. She helps
Genevieve get a small glass of milk. They sit at the small,
round, dining table. Neither one talks but Gen quietly hums
to herself. Finally, when Gen finishes her cup, she jumps

down. She attempts to put her empty glass in the sink but fails. Before the glass hits the floor, Julia jumps to her feet and she snatches the small child away from the falling cup. After the loud crash, Gen begins to cry.

"Sorry, sorry, sorry, sorry, sorry." She continuously mumbles between sobs.

Julia gives the crying girl a huge bear hug. With her arms still around Gen, Julia spins around in a circle. She can hear a combination of laughing and crying from Gen. After a several minutes longer of both tears and giggles, Julia sits Gen on the table, wiping her eyes with her sleeve.

"Gen-Gen, stop crying. It's ok! Accidents happen. I've broken many dishes before." Julia notices Genevieve doesn't seem relieved by the news so she continues, "See?" She holds up her arm. To the left of a tattooed butterfly is a large scar on her forearm. When I was little, I grabbed a plate but it slipped out of my hand. It smashed on the floor. I tried to catch it before it hit the floor and that's how I cut myself."

"Was Grandma mad at you?"

"She didn't like that I didn't listen to her but she wasn't mad that I broke her plate."

A thought occurs to Genevieve. It brings a quick smile through her tears. "Is Grandma here?"

Julia's mind immediately jumps to the state she found her mother in a couple hours before. Not wanting her niece to see her own family the way she'd seen her, she quickly says, "Oh, Grandma wasn't feeling well and went to bed."

"Did she have too much juice too?"

Julia looks away so Gen can't see the puzzled look on her face. "Is that what happened to Momma? She had too much juice again?"

"Yep. You right, Aunt Jul. I am getting sleepy. Wanna read me a story?"

"You got it, kiddo. Go grab your blanket from my room. I'm going to grab your pajamas from the bathroom."

She lets out a sigh of relief and watches the little girl scamper away. Julia heads to the bathroom to grab some PJs from the bathroom closet. She flips on the light and looks around. What she can only assume are dirty towels and clothes litter the floor. She quickly gathers them up into a large pile. In a brown, woven basket in the corner of the bathroom, Julia locates the fuzzy, blue jammies near the top of the pile. She puts them over her shoulder to free her hands. She puts the towels in the clothes hamper and walks back into the living room. There is no sign of Genevieve. She walks to her bedroom. After turning on the light in the room, she notices that Gen's blanket is missing.

"She must have grabbed it," Julia mumbles sleepily to herself. She exits the room, turning off the light. When she doesn't see Gen in the living room, she glances toward the only other room in the house. The door to her mother's room is ajar. Remembering previously, the door was shut completely, Julia panics. She walks quickly but as quietly as possible to the opened door. Even with the light off, Julia could see a tiny silhouette standing next to the bed.

The light from the living room casts a low glow on Gen's grandma's sleeping face. Her eyes appear to be squeezed shut and a small circle of drool pools next to her open mouth. Beads of sweat help mat her hair to her cheek and fore-head. Julia decides not to turn on a light but instead turns to Genevieve. She grabs her hand and gently leads her out of the room.

Once they get into the living room, Gen runs to the couch and jumps onto it. Settling herself down in her favor-ite spot, she curls up into a tiny ball Julia lies down next to her and looks at the front of the book. It's a book of nursery rhymes her grandmother had given her. Julia turns to Gen and smiles. Julia starts at the first page and begins reading slowly. After each page, she takes another glance at Genevieve to see if she's sleeping yet. After getting through more than half of the children's book, Gen's eye finally close. A wisp of hair has fallen in front of her face and it moves in sync with her breathing. Julia brushes it away. She sits up and slowly gets off the couch. She looks at Gen for a second to make sure she is completely asleep. She stretches her aching body. Unsure now of what to do, she walks back into the kitchen. She quickly checks the floor for more glass. Thankful to come up empty, she cleans up the rest of the kitchen. After wiping down the counters, cleaning the dirty dishes, scrubbing the oven and taking out the trash, she grabs a small glass of milk for herself. She drinks it fast then places the dirty cup in the sink. With the kitchen now sparkling clean, Julia checks on Gen. Her eyes are closed and her deep, slow breathing tell Julia that she's still fast asleep. Julia gives her a quick kiss on her forehead and wraps the blanket around her tightly. She enters her own room, realizing for the first time how exhausted she really is. She is about to crawl into her bed but stops. She disappointingly remembers that it is unmade. Her mother had taken all her sheets and blankets off to wash them. They have not been returned. Julia assumes they have disappeared like everything else Jossa touches. She stands in the middle of her room with her eyes closed, willing the strength needed to find the blankets before exhaustion totally takes over.

Julia cracks open Jossa's bedroom door. She listens to make sure she hears her mother's heavy breathing, too. She makes her way to the closet door and quietly opens it. Something falls out, hitting her foot. "Ouch!" she can't help but shout out. She pauses to listen for her mother's breathing, again, hoping her loud yelp didn't wake her up. When she finally hears it again, she begins blindly digging through the closet. She reaches into the back of the closet and her hands fall onto a soft blanket. She grabs the pile of blankets, still trying hard to stay quiet. As she nears the bedroom door, a particularly foul smell stops her. She turns around to her mother but the darkness of the room prevents her from seeing anything. Without another second thought, she turns on the light. It takes a second for her eyes to adjust to the sudden brightness. Curled up in a tight ball, in the fetal position, her mother lays in the middle of the bed. From the top of her head to her stomach is covered in vomit.

Julia tries to keep herself from heaving as she drops the blanket and runs to her mother.

"Mom, wake up!" Julia begins shaking her mother. Finally, very slowly, Jossa rolls over onto her back and her eyes open.

"W-what?"

"Mom, you need to get up. You threw up everywhere. Get up. Let's go take a shower."

"No, I'm so tired. I'm just gonna go back to sleep."

"No, you are not. Get up," Julia says harshly. "You need to get cleaned up. I'm going to start a shower for you. Seriously, get up," she says again as she heads out of the room.

Julia leaves the room and walks into the bathroom. She quickly turns on the light and runs the shower. She purposely makes the shower colder than usual. Before she walks back into the bedroom, she walks over to Gen and makes sure she's still sleeping. Gen's eyes are still closed and the blankets are still tucked tightly around her. Julia smiles. She slowly walks back into the bedroom. Her mother is still lying on the bed.

"Mom!" Jossa rolls over, covering her eyes with her arms. Julia reaches over and grabs her arm. "Ok, that's enough. Let's go." Julia pulls a very drunk, Jossa, to her feet. Although it is a major struggle, she helps her stumble into the bathroom. Jossa throws herself onto the toilet and places her head onto the adjacent sink.

"Nope," Julia says. "Stand up," Julia forces her half-conscious mother to stand up. Julia helps her remove her clothes and step into the freezing cold shower. As soon as the water hits her face, Jossa gasps and stumbles backward. Luckily, Julia is there and grabs her mom's arm to steady her.

"Look at me," Julia says. "Mom, look at me."

With drunken eyes, Jossa looks over to Julia but doesn't say a word.

"I'm going to be right back. I need you to just stand her. Do not move. Do you understand me?"

Jossa nods her head but doesn't speak.

Taking that as a yes, Julia shuts the shower curtain. She walks out of the bathroom, shutting the door halfway. She walks into her mother's room. The stench is beginning to worsen. Julia quickly strips the bed of the sheets and blankets. She looks in the closet for extra sheets. Finding only a small blanket, Julia puts it on the bare mattress. Unable to find another larger blanket to use as a cover, Julia grabs the heap of blanket she'd left by the door. As she picks it up, she hears a small *clang*, as something hits the wooden floor. She looks down at the floor. A small handgun lays on the floor, glistening in the light of the bedroom. Julia panics and grabs the gun from the floor. She runs into her own room and throws it in her sock drawer. As she shuts the drawer, a loud crash resonates from the bathroom.

Julia hurriedly leaves her room and runs into the bathroom. Jossa is lying on the floor, looking up at the ceiling, and her feet are dangling over the side of the tub.

"Mom, what happened?" Julia breathlessly asks.

Jossa doesn't respond but Julia has already guessed. "Did ya fall? Are you alright?" Jossa still doesn't answer. "Let's get you into bed."

Julia helps her mother into a pair of flannel pants and a t-shirt. She guides her mother back into her bedroom. Jossa collapses onto her bed. Julia pulls the blanket up over her mother. Before Julia has a chance to leave the room, Jossa has fallen asleep. The loud snoring is the last thing Julia hears as she closes the door. She crawls, once again, into her unmade bed. This time, however, she doesn't notice the chill. Her eyes close and she drifts off to sleep for a second time.

The next morning, Julia awakens to her alarm clock. The buzzing startles her for a second or two. Once her racing heart calms down, she looks down beside her. Snuggled in a small ball next to her is Genevieve. Julia tries to remember when she came in but most of the night was a blur. She wakes up the sleeping beauty by wrapping her arm around her and kissing her cheek. Gen sleepily giggles and rubs her face and eyes.

"Good morning, Gen-Gen."

Genevieve rolls over and snuggles closer to Julia.

"Want some breakfast?" Julia asks, still more than half-asleep herself.

"No," Genevieve mumbles. "Sleep," she continues.

Julia looks at the clock next to her bed. Realizing it is time for her to wake up and get ready for school, she forces herself out of what is now a very warm bed. She shivers as she walks to the kitchen. She can't stop herself from yawning several times. Without much thought, she begins making scrambled eggs and toast. She goes through the motions of setting out plates and pouring juice. When breakfast is finally ready, she goes back in to get Gen out of bed.

"Alright, munchkin, time to get up. Breakfast is ready."

Genevieve reluctantly and slowly climbs out of bed. She grabs her blanket and wraps it around herself. Julia follows Gen out of the room and back into the tiny kitchen. Gen climbs into her favorite chair while Julia grabs the skillet of eggs. She dishes out a small portion and slides a small glass of juice next to her. Once Gen is settled and begins eating, Julia walks into her mother's bedroom. She turns on the light but Jossa does not move a muscle. With no patience left for her mother, Julia takes off her mother's blankets and says, "Alright, get up. Breakfast is ready."

Jossa groans loudly. "My head hurts. Can you get me something for it?"

"Sure," Julia says unemotionally. "Genevieve is here and she wants to say hi. I made breakfast so why don't you get up."

"What about my pills?"

Placing her hands on her hips, Julia says with authority, "You can have some but you've got to get out of bed first."

Without another word, Jossa gets out of bed. She sways slightly before gathering her bearings. Her hair is still wet from last night's shower. After she stands up, Jossa looks back down at the bed.

"Where are my blankets?"

Julia walks out of the room. This is a regular occurrence so there is no need to explain anything. She walks out into the kitchen and begins refilling Gen's plate with more eggs.

"Thank you." Gen looks up at her aunt and smiles.

Julia smiles back. "You are welcome, Gen-Gen. Do you want more juice?"

"Yeah." Julia gives her a disapproving look and Gen fixes her statement. "Yes, please."

Julia smiles again. "Good job. Here you go." She passes the now full cup back towards Gen.

"Grandma!" Gen screeches. She hops down from her chair and runs to a still very hungover Jossa.

Jossa bends down and gives the little girl a quick hug. "Go eat, sweetheart." Gen runs back to her seat and climbs in. No one talks to each other during the rest of the breakfast. As they finish eating, Julia hears the sharp knock on her the front door. Everyone jumps to their feet.

"I got it, sit down," Julia says to the rest of the group. She walks into the living room. The loud knocking continues. More irritated than curious who is at the door, Julia unlocks the door and opens it.

"HHHEEEYYYY!" A very loud, young woman shouts. Without an invitation, the woman pushes passed Julia and throws herself onto the couch. Seeing the blankets, she asks, "Did you have someone over last night? Was it a man?"

"Yeah, I had someone over…your daughter. Thank you for dropping her off and letting me know."

"Oh, you're welcome. You like watching her so I didn't think you'd mind. How's she doing?"

"Mommy!" Gen's voice echoes through the room. She dashes toward her mother, throwing her arms around her neck.

"Hey you. Are you done eating, peanut?" Anni asks noticing the food on her daughter's face.

"Nope."

Julia interjects. "Hey, Gen. Why don't you go finish eating. I have to get ready to go soon."

"Where are you going?" Anni asks. "I was hoping you could watch Gen today."

"No, I can't."

"But I have plans today. Can't you watch her for awhile?" Looking down at Gen, Anni continues, "Gen, wouldn't you like to play with Aunt Julia today?"

"No, Anni. Don't do that. I need to go to school and I have work afterwards. I'm going to be late as it is. Take care of your own child for once. I'm serious. I can't watch her."

"I can't believe you're acting like this. I never ask you for anything. When I do, you won't help me out. That's crazy. You act like you are so high and mighty now that you've got a job. You work at a stupid deli only a couple nights a week. I'd have a job too if I didn't have a kid."

Having heard a similar rant from her irresponsible sister before, Julia unsympathetically crosses her arms. "I don't care. I watched her all night. I haven't gotten any sleep and now I have school to go to."

"Thanks for nothing, I guess." Anni gets to her feet and walks into the kitchen. Although Julia doesn't move from her spot in the living room, she can hear Anni talking to her daughter.

"Hurry up, let's go. We need to go home."

Within minutes, they both emerge back into the living room. Julia kneels down onto the floor and outstretches her arms. Gen runs to her, giggling as she runs. She dives into Julia's arms. After giving Gen a few kisses, Julia stands up.

"You better be good, ok? I'll see you later. I love you."

"Love you, Aunt Juls."

As soon as the door shuts, Julia runs into her room and changes into her raggedy school clothes. She leaves her pajamas on the floor and shuts the door. She walks into the kitchen to say good-bye to her mom, however, Jossa is passed out with her head on the table. Rolling her eyes, Julia double checks to make sure the stove is turned off and the toaster is unplugged. She leaves her mother in the kitchen and exits the apartment. Although it is still somewhat dark outside, Julia walks the five blocks to her school. As she walks up the front steps of the over-crowded school, she prays for the strength to stay awake and get through the day.

MARK

Mark looks down at his cell phone screen. For the second time in ten minutes, he brushes his hair out of his eyes. He checks his teeth in the camera. When he is once again satisfied with his appearance, he blacks out the screen and looks up. His date is sitting across the table, staring curiously at him.

"So, Graciela," Mark says. "Tell me something I don't already know about you."

"Well, I really don't like my job. I've worked there …"

"Hey, guys, what are we drinking tonight?" The short, stocky waitress holds a small, black notepad.

Mark quickly makes his decision based on listening to the types of beers available. Graciela, however, takes much longer. Tapping his fingers on the table, Mark takes a deep breath and loudly blows it out. Graciela looks up at him. Mark stops tapping on the table. He's relieved when she finally orders a water with both a quartered lemon and lime. As the waitress walks away, Mark turns his gaze to her; watching her leave.

A stern voice clears her throat. Mark turns back to face Graciela.

"Did you enjoy yourself?"

"What? Oh yeah. I mean … no. Sorry, what were you saying?"

Graciela pauses for a minute. "I don't know," she says. "I'm sure it isn't important."

"Do you have any brothers or sisters?"

She grumpily responds. "I have four brothers and three sisters." After seeing the shocked look on Mark's face, she continues, "My mother was a very busy woman."

Mark leans his head on his hand. "Wow, that's amazing. I only have an older brother but I don't see much of him anymore. He's in jail. Do you get along with all of them?"

She lets out a small chuckle. "No. I actually only speak to one of them. We had a hard life growing up and all of us dealt with it differently."

"How so?"

The young woman seems a little taken aback by the prying. "Wow, ummm…this is our first date. Let's save some things for date number two."

"Oh, come on. I'll give you some good gossip about my family." Mark sits back and tries to make the conversation seem more casual. "I bet mine's worse than yours, anyway."

Mark sees the appalled look on Graciela's face. Trying to switch gears, he leans forward and says, "Well, what have your other boyfriends been like? I think I, at least, deserve to know that."

"So," she hesitantly begins. "This is supposed to be a get-to-know-you sort of date. You don't…"

Although Graciela cuts her sentence short, Mark doesn't realize it. His head is down and his eyes are transfixed onto the screen of his phone. He is furiously texting his friend. Finding himself getting lost in the conversation, he is startled when there is a loud knocking on the table. He finally looks up from the screen.

"What?" he asks rudely. "I was listening to you."

"What was I saying, then?" Graciela spats back.

"You were saying something about your boyfriend and how you broke up."

Graciela rolls her eyes. "Since we're apparently playing a game of twenty questions, let me ask you a question. How old are you?"

Mark grins at her question. It is a question he's received many times and his answer just flows out of him without thinking. "Twenty-eight," he lies. "Is that alright with you?"

Looking slightly unsure, Graciela hesitantly responds, "Yeah, I guess. No offense, though, but you look a lot older than twenty-eight. Hope that doesn't offend you," she adds quickly.

"Well, you should see me when I don't dye my hair. Hahaha."

Unfortunately, he's the only person laughing at his own joke. Graciela doesn't crack a smile. "You know what," she says decidedly. "I don't think this is a good idea." She stands up, throwing her cloth napkin on the table. "I gave this a chance but I think it's time for me to go."

"We haven't ordered food yet!" Mark shouts in a panic.

Graciela looks at Mark. "Good," she says. "Then the bill won't be too high."

"Odd," he hears her mumble as she turns back around.

As soon as she's out of sight, Mark puts his elbows on the table and drops his head into his hand. The anger inside of him is brewing. How did such a potentially nice evening turn completely sour? He pounds his hands onto the table loudly enough that several other couples around him look in his direction. He pulls out his smart phone from his pocket. Unsure of what to do now, he attempts to call his friend, Tom, to inform him of what occurred with Graciela. After three full rings, the voicemail is the only answer Mark gets from Tom.

"Hey. You're right. She bailed. I may need to adjust my age. She didn't buy the whole 'I'm twenty-eight' nonsense. Oh well. I need a beer." He hangs up. Grabbing the large glass of beer on the table, he drinks it as fast as he can. After finishing his last gulp, he slams the cup onto the table. He begins to saunter toward the exit, leaving the check untouched.

He throws his jean jacket over his shoulder and as he reaches the front door, he turns around and winks at the young hostess. She barely smiles in return. He walks out into the cool evening air. The once full parking lot is now only half full at best. He walks to his brand new, forest green jeep. Although the walk to his vehicle is short, with every step he takes, his anger increases. By the time he arrives to the driver side door, his anger boils over. He thrusts the door open, banging the side of the car next to him. The large scratch left on the car doesn't faze him. When he turns on the engine, loud rap music blasts him in the face. He sits for a second or two before using his pent up anger to punch the steering wheel. During his tantrum, his phone rings. He glances at it. It's Tom.

"Thanks for answering your phone," Mark says.

He quickly tells him the story of his date. Once he finishes, Tom invites him to a house party his cousin is hosting. Mark makes plans to pick up his friend at his house in half an hour. With his horrible mood somewhat lifted, Mark revs his engine before pulling out of the dark parking lot. He reaches under the front seat and pulls out a small bottle of vodka. He quickly removes the cap and takes several large swigs. Taking his hands off the wheel, he replaces the lid and throws it onto the passenger seat of the car. He grabs the wheels again just in time to stop it from careening toward oncoming traffic. He races through many residential allotments smirking as he passes the posted speed limit signs-too low for his taste. Ten minutes later, he arrives at Tom's duplex. He thrusts his jeep into park and jumps out. He pounds on the front door, impatiently waiting for someone to open it. After another round of pounding, the front door finally swings open. A young woman wearing skimpy, tight clothes answers the door. She is holding a beer bottle in one hand and a toddler in another. This catches Mark off guard.

"Oh! Hello." Mark says. "Where's Tom?"

The woman adjusts the child on the side of her body and Mark can hear her sigh loudly. She steps aside to allow Mark to enter the small living room, however, she doesn't answer

Mark's question. The couple continues to stand in the cluttered room, staring at one another. Finally, Mark breaks the increasingly awkward silence.

"Tom. Where is he?"

As though appearing to be surprised by the question, the woman stutters, "Oh, ummm, I don't know."

She turns around and leaves the room without another word. He can hear the young child crying but it is muffled by the sounds of a loud television. Mark goes straight to the kitchen. He yanks the refrigerator door open. He grabs two cans of beer, slams the door shut, and walks back into the living room. He throws himself onto a small, brown couch. The stuffing is slowly falling out and stains cover the cushions. He places his feet on the small coffee table sitting in front of the couch. It creaks loudly; even under such little weight. He pops both cans open. Double fisting the beers, he finishes both cans in mere minutes. He smashes them as small as he can and tosses them onto the coffee table next to several others. Just then, Tom walks into the room.

"What's up?"

"You look ready to go out," Mark says sarcastically. The man standing in the living room is wearing nothing more than a pair of red and white boxer shorts. His hair sits messily on the top of his head and he's wearing thick, black, rimmed glasses. "I don't think I've ever seen you without contacts," Mark laughs. "You look dumb."

"Shut it."

"Hurry up! We ain't going anywhere with you looking like that. You need to be my wing man tonight!"

"You really want to go out? I just figured you were upset about your successful date." Tom grins at Mark. Feeling his anger begin to boil, again, Mark grabs a half empty can of beer sitting on the coffee table and chucks it at Tom. It hits Tom, bouncing off his chest. Tom laughs and exits the room. Getting comfortable on the couch, Mark grabs the remote.

He tries to change the channel but is unsuccessful. After a few failed attempts, he becomes frustrated and throws the remote across the room. It smacks the far wall and falls to the floor in two pieces. Upon hearing the commotion, the woman walks back into the room.

"What did you do?" She stands in the doorway with her hands crossed across her chest.

"Your remote doesn't work. I thought if I threw it against the wall, it may work."

The woman takes a quick look across the room and spots the broken remote. She purses her lips tightly together and furrows her brow. She shakes her head and says, "You idiot, it just needs batteries. Tom took them out 'cause he needed them for something else. Ridiculous." She turns around and heads back to the bathroom.

Minutes later, Tom emerges. He is wearing jeans with holes in both knees. His red flannel shirt and dark brown shoes add the finishing touches to his attire.

"So, who's the chick?" Mark asks Tom, regarding the strange, young woman.

"No one important," Tom says bluntly. "Let's go."

"Hold on," Mark says, getting to his feet. He trots back into the kitchen and grabs two more beers from the fridge. The couple head out of the door. Mark is halfway to his car when Tom's phone rings.

"Damn it!" Tom shouts, "I'll be right back."

Mark watches as Tom walks over to the garage and disappears. Unsure of what to do while he waits, Mark climbs into the passenger side of Tom's car. He opens the center console and is relieved when he finds an amber vial lying neatly on top. He plucks it out and without a second thought, tosses several of the tablets inside, into his mouth. He washes it down with an entire can of beer. After a few minutes of sitting in the car by himself, he grows impatient. He leans over to the steering wheel and blasts the horn for several seconds.

Tom emerges from the darkness. As he nears the car, Mark can see the anger in his face. Tom punches the hood of his own car before climbing into the driver side seat

"I'm assuming your talk went well, huh?" Mark says.

"Change of plans," Tom responds. He pulls quickly out of the gravel driveway, kicking up stones as they go.

After ten minutes or more of silence, Mark asks, "So, what's going on? You better not be ruining my night."

"Dude, shut up."

"Dude, screw you. Where are we going?"

"I'm not going to let my stupid girlfriend break up with me for some other loser."

"Maybe she realized she didn't want a boyfriend with gray hair," Mark boldly states.

Tom glares at his longtime friend. "You should talk. Nobody is going to believe you're twenty-eight. You're lucky she didn't ask to see your driver's license."

"Alright, point made. Graciela was beautiful, though."

"Meagan is at some party with another dude. She told me she was doing a school project. We need to take care of this."

"That's what you get for dating a high school student."

"She's not in high school." He pauses. "Ok, well, I guess technically she's in high school but that's because she got held back a couple of times. Regardless, she's cheating on me and I'll be damned if I let that happen."

"I need another beer, anyway."

The rest of the trip, although short, is done in silence. Once they arrive on the street, there is no question which house is hosting the party. Tom parks the car on the side of the road. He quickly jumps out, forgetting to shut the car door. Mark sighs. He slowly climbs out and watches his friend stomp towards the house. He stretches his sore muscles. Instead of following his friend, he approaches a small group of girls. He smiles confidently and brushes the long strands of hair from his eyes.

"Hey ladies, how's it going?" He flashes a large smile in their direction.

At first, no one acknowledges him. They continue their conversation, laughing and drinking bottles of beer. When the group realizes the strange intruder isn't going away, the woman closest to him speaks. "Can I help you?"

"Sure, my name is Mark. I wanted to come over and introduce myself to the prettiest bunch of women at this party."

"I'm Ashley and unfortunately, we're not interested in dating a grandpa."

Mark can feel his face become flushed with anger. He balls up his fists. "Grandpa, huh?" Mark takes a step toward the outgoing young woman and forcefully kisses her. She struggles against him, trying to free herself. He lets go after a few seconds.

"What's wrong with you?" Ashley does her best to push him away. "Don't let my boyfriend catch you touching me. He'll kill you. Come on, guys, let's go inside."

She leads her posse into the house. Mark watches her walk away and he shakes his head. He looks around the yard, trying to locate Tom. Not seeing him out front, he walks inside the front door as well. He does his best to avoid the group of girls. Looking around the room, he feels slightly out of place. This is clearly a high school party and a thirty-five year old man sticks out like a sore thumb. Speaking of thumb, he looks down at his hands. They have begun to shake. He opens and closes his hands several times. He makes his way into a small kitchen where the beer is located. He grabs two of them from the refrigerator. He downs them within minutes. He grabs another one and as he opens it, a loud commotion startles him. Everyone in the kitchen runs out into the living room. Curious, Mark sips his beer and slowly walks out of the kitchen, following the crowds of people. The noise is coming from outside and it grows louder and louder as he gets closer. When Mark gets to the doorway, he sees the cause for the noise. It is coming from the large circle in the middle of the dark yard. The cheering and screaming are for the two people in the middle of the growing circle. As Mark nears the group, two guys are throwing punches at one another. Standing on the other end of the circle is a young woman that looks oddly familiar. Her screams seem to echo through the already loud crowd.

"Stop it! Jason, stop!" Her screams go unanswered as the fight continues.

Mark can't stop himself from staring at her. He racks his brain trying to remember where he'd seen her before. Then it dawns on him. This is Tom's girlfriend. He runs to the circle of people, spilling some of his beer onto the lawn. He approaches the crowd and pushes his way through until he is able to clearly see the fight. Sure enough, Tom is one of the people in the center ring. Getting caught up in the fight, Mark begins cheering the guys on.

After a few minutes, the fight comes to an abrupt end when a small framed body falls to the ground. The cheering stops, too. Tom walks around the body, throwing his arms in the air in triumph. Meagan runs over to Tom, shoving him as hard as she can. He barely flinches. He is undeterred by the lack of cheering and continues to walk around the limp body.

Mark jumps up and down, celebrating with Tom. Meagan runs over to Jason. He is slowly coming to. The crowd disperses and only a few people remain in the backyard. Meagan is knelt down next to Jason, who is now sitting up.

"Why did you do that?" Meagan shouts.

"Are you kidding me? You stupid idiot, you're cheating on me. What did you expect? I kicked his ass 'cause I can't kick yours!" Tom takes a few steps toward Jason. Jason unsteadily gets to his feet. Blood pours out of his busted nose and his right eye is already beginning to swell.

"We are not together anymore!" Meagan shouts at Tom.

Jason looks bewildered at Meagan. "You...you dated this guy? He is old enough to be your dad!"

The comment sends both Tom and Mark into a rage.

"No!" Meagan shouts, jumping in front of her boyfriend. "Leave him alone!"

Tom manages to get one swift kick that connect with Jason's shin.

"Alright," Mark says. "Let's get out of here."

Tom doesn't say another word but turns around and heads to the front of the house. Once there, he quickly walks to his car and gets in. Mark has to walk fast to keep up with his friend. Once they both get into Tom's small car, Mark says, "Well, that was a great party. I hope this other party is just as fun." Tom turns and opens his mouth to respond. Mark doesn't allow this. "Tom, what is wrong with you? I know you're a jerk but that's..." Mark pauses. "That's more than I expected. It was awesome, though."

The pair arrive at another house party. There is a noticeable difference in the two parties. The biggest difference is in the age of the crowd. They are thankfully much older than the high school party. Tom hasn't had an opportunity to turn the car off before people race toward them. Ten or more people run up to the car, pounding on the hood. Tom throws open the driver side door, laughing and shoving people off of his car.

"Where's my drink?" Mark asks between laughs.

A man, slightly younger than both Tom and Mark shoves an ice cold beer into his hand.

"Where have you been?" another guy shouts at the pair.

"Dude, John, we both have had a horrible night. "Let..."

The man interrupts Mark by saying, "For every time you complain, you have to take a shot."

"Sounds good to me!" Tom says.

Mark yells to the group, "In that case, my day sucks!" He begins to chug the beer in his hand. When he finishes it, he smashes the can against his forehead and throws it onto the ground.

"Alright, I'm ready for another one!"

Several people cheer. Without another word, Mark leads Tom to the house. Before Mark gets to the front door, a small fog of green smoke greets him. Catching himself coughing, he continues walking inside. He looks around, trying to find the path to the kitchen. He steps over groups of people making out on the floor. Finally, he reaches the kitchen. On the counter are several types of strong liquor. He takes out a bottle of vodka and pours some into a blue plastic cup. He downs the drink as though it's water.

"You gonna pour me some or do I have to do it myself?"

Mark looks over and is surprised to see a petite, young woman staring at him. He smiles at her and quickly grabs another cup. He pours the cup more than half full and hands it to the woman. "You're not really gonna drink all of that, are you?" he challenges her.

"Game on," she says mischievously.

They both begin drinking while not breaking eye contact. Mark is the first one to take a break. As soon as Mark slams his cup down onto the counter, the woman slowly lowers hers.

They lock eyes.

"Wanna amp up this lame party?"

Intrigued, Mark smiles. "Of course."

Mark watches as the woman reaches into the pocket of her jeans. She pulls out several pills. She smiles and hands 3 pills to Mark.

"Ready?" she whispers.

Mark nods.

"1-2-3."

Mark throws the pills back into his mouth, chasing the pills with a large swallow of vodka.

PART II

ELIZABETH

The house, usually loud with two screaming toddlers, is finally quiet. Elizabeth leans back into her favorite easy chair. She lays the book she's reading onto her chest, unsure if she should keep reading or just take a nap. She still has so much to do around the house before Andrew gets home from picking up the girls. Exhaustion takes over and Elizabeth finds her eyes closing. Just before she drifts off to sleep, the phone rings. She quickly stretches and climbs to her feet. She feels a little unsteady. She lazily and slowly staggers to the small side table in her room. She grabs the tiny cell phone on the fourth ring.

"Hello?" she quietly asks.

"What are you doing right now?" a low, male voice asks.

Slightly taken aback by this, Elizabeth says the first thing that comes to mind. "Well, I'm clearly talking to you. Who is this?"

"Who I am is not important. Do you know what is important, though?"

"What?" she says, taking the bait.

"Do you know where your children are?"

Elizabeth's heart plummets to her toes. Without a second thought, she quickly hangs up the phone. She races down the hall toward the toddlers' room. She throws open the half-closed door. Although, from the doorway, she can clearly see two masses lying in their toddler beds, she walks in and checks both girls. Maddie is curled up in a small ball while Maria lays outstretched in the bed next to her. She's clutching tightly to her blanket. Elizabeth makes sure both girls are breathing and she lets out a sigh of relief. Once she's calmed down, she checks every square inch of the room. After a few minutes, she feels confident that not only is no one in the room but the window is both shut and locked. Elizabeth quietly leaves the room, surprised she manages to not wake the girls.

She wanders back into her own room. The more she thinks about the phone call, the angrier she becomes. Who would call her and say something so horrible? Maybe it was just a wrong number. Her mind jumps to the week prior. She received a chillingly similar phone call claiming to be watching the house. Unsure of what exactly to do, she picks up the phone and calls her husband. He doesn't answer. She is becoming increasingly anxious from her phone call so she leaves a frantic voicemail.

"Honey, listen, some man just called me. He asked what I was doing," she's getting choked up thinking about it. "He asked me where my children are. I checked on them and both girls are fine. Actually, I don't know if I locked the front door so I'm going to go. Call me, please. I love you, honey."

She quickly hangs up the phone and runs downstairs and straight to the front door. She looks through the peephole and when she doesn't see anyone, she locks the door and deadbolts it. Still very shaken from the strange man, she picks the phone back up and dials her husband's work number again. After the second ring, the familiar voice answers.

"What is it now?"

"Can you come home? I don't think we should be home by ourselves right now."

"Elizabeth, you know I can't do that. Calm down, ok? Everything is fine." As an afterthought, he asks, "The girls are fine, right?"

"Yeah, they're fine. But listen, Andrew, you can come home if you really want to. I don't understand why you don't."

"Just because I run the company, doesn't mean I can just leave whenever I want to. People expect me to be here."

"I expect you to be *here*," Elizabeth emphasizes.

"Elizabeth, I can't come home. Why don't you take the girls and go visit my mother. They haven't seen their grandmother in awhile, anyway."

"But…" she starts to say but realizes it's pointless. "Okay," she says, defeated.

"I'm going to go. Try to relax and I'll be home soon."

Liar, she wants to say but stops. She forces herself to smile through her teeth and tells her husband good-bye.

Feeling her face getting red and her heart begin to beat faster, Elizabeth hangs up the phone. She walks into the kitchen and grabs a cup of juice from the fridge. She sips the juice, trying to decide whether to check on the girls again. She decides she's only going to feel better if she does. She very slowly and as quietly as possible, opens their bedroom door. The room is dark from the pulled curtains. She hears only the quiet, steady breathing of two sleeping twins. She sneaks up to their beds. They are still snuggled up tightly. She takes a second to appreciate the view. She bends down and gives each girl a small kiss on their forehead. As quietly as she entered, she exits; closing the door once more behind her.

The phone rings. She jumps. Instinctively, she turns toward her own bedroom; the closest room with a phone. Then the memory of her last phone call comes flooding back to her. She ignores the call. If there is anything important, the caller will just leave a message, she thinks hopefully to herself. The phone continues to ring two more times before the answering machine picks it up. Elizabeth waits for the message. The only message is light breathing. Panicking, Elizabeth grabs the answering machine and yanks it out of the wall. The breathing disappears. As she holds the machine in her tiny hands, she realizes what she did. She's very disappointed in herself. She's always been one to control her emotions under all circumstances. Not today, however.

The phone downstairs rings again. Elizabeth begins to shake uncontrollably now. Tears begin to cloud her vision. She walks into her children's room. In the darkness, she finds a small section of empty wall space near the bed. She leans against the wall and slides down to the floor. She brings her knees to her chest and head to her knees. She closes her eyes as the phone continues to ring. She sobs quietly while her girls sleep.

• • •

"Let's go! Hurry up, girls!"

Elizabeth stands in the doorway of her daughters' bedroom. Although she tries to play off a calm demeanor, panic has long set in. The girls attempt to put on their shoes by themselves. Elizabeth can feel her anxiety growing as she watches her children take their time getting dressed.

"Ok, here," Elizabeth quickly walks into their room. "Let me help you."

She kneels down onto the floor and quickly slides each foot into their individual shoe and tightly buckles it. She plasters on her biggest yet fakest smile. "Are you ready to go, girls?"

"Yeah!" Both girls squeal with delight, jump up from their carpeted bedroom floor, and race down the stairs. Elizabeth is only a couple steps behind. They all pile into the car and Elizabeth helps both girls get properly buckled. They pull out of the driveway and head toward the park. They listen and sing to a handful of songs from their favorite CD. Elizabeth notices her mood lifting as they pull into one of the few available parking spots. Once the car is in park, Elizabeth takes a deep breath.

"Out now, Mommy?"

Elizabeth can barely turn around with her seat belt on. "Yeah, sweetheart. We can get out." She smiles.

She quickly unbuckles her seatbelt, hops out of the driver seat, and quickly opens the back door. She unbuckles both girls and they excitedly jump down and bolt towards the slides.

"Be careful!" she yells to their retreating backs.

She takes her time getting her purse out of the passenger seat and shutting all the doors. She walks slowly to the benches that surround the playground. The playground is busier than usual. She sits down next to another woman. This woman is nearly twice her age. Elizabeth gives her a small smile. She sits back and makes herself comfortable on the bench and watches her girls running around the mulched playground. She sighs heavily and checks her watch. Andrew won't be home for several more hours. Cold chills run up and down her spine and she outwardly shivers.

"You ok, dear?"

Elizabeth quickly turns to her bench mate. The older woman is looking at Elizabeth with kind eyes.

"Yeah, I'm fine." Elizabeth tries to keep her voice from shaking. "Thanks," she adds when she can still feel the woman's eyes on her. Unable to take the staring any longer, she gets to her feet and slowly walks around to the sandbox. Maddie is completely covered in sand. Elizabeth chuckles when she sees the sight. Maria is pouring bucket after bucket full of sand on top of her sister's head. When Maddie finally had enough of her sand bath, she leaps up, shakes off the excessive sand, and pounces on Maria. They laugh and giggle and continue to tackle each other in the tiny, black rubber box.

"Those two silly girls yours?"

The trance Elizabeth found herself in is immediately broken. Hanging on her left arm is the woman from the bench. She's a bit surprised at being followed. "Oh, yeah. The one in the pink is Maria and Maddie is in the blue. Do you have kids here?" Elizabeth tries to sound sincere. Although she's not sure if it is successful, the woman seems content with the flow of the conversation.

"Well, sort of. I'm Grandma. Just doing a little babysitting for my daughter."

"Oh, that's nice."

"Yeah, it's been fun." The woman pauses. "Truthfully, it's been exhausting."

"Oh, I completely understand that. Which is your grandkid?"

She chuckles. "The rambunctious two over by the swings are my daughter's kids."

"Do you mean the two that are wrestling in the gravel?"

The woman leans forward and squints. "Oh, yes. That's them."

"Well, I'm sure they're delightful kids."

"Sometimes. The youngest one is over there by the slide." She scans the playground. "I'm missing one. Oh there he is," she points next to the sandbox where the twins are playing.

"You're watching four kids?! Wow! That's impressive."

"Just trying to wear them out."

"Well, that's a good idea."

"So, I hate to keep prodding but are you sure you're ok, dear? You seem very upset when you got here."

Elizabeth ponders for a moment. She's unsure how honest to be with her new acquaintance. She looks over at her children. They're laughing and running around. They keep running back to the sandbox and throwing handfuls of sand at each other. Maria slips and falls onto the mulch and bursts into tears. Elizabeth takes several steps toward her but before she gets too close, she stops. Maddie rushes over and helps her to her feet. Maddie lovingly wipes the tears from her sister's dirty cheek. Elizabeth smiles. The more she thinks about her elusive phone call, the more she wonders if she had over reacted. It wouldn't take very much investigating to know she had children. The toys in the front yard would be an instant give away.

"Oh, just had a long day. You're right, children can be exhausting."

She doesn't make eye contact with the woman. She keeps looking forward but she can feel those same set of eyes boring into her. After a several uncomfortable minutes, the woman walks toward her own children and Elizabeth can hear her yelling for them.

"Max and Benjamin, Anna, Eli! Come on, let's get ready to go!"

Elizabeth walks back over to the bench so she can comfortably watch her children. They are now playing by the yellow slides. They are nicely taking turns and gently pushing each other down. She can hear them giggle with laughter. Her heart swells with love. She reaches down into her large tote bag and pulls out a plastic water bottle. She takes several swigs from it. Before she gets the bottle back into her bag, her phone rings. The caller ID says "*Hubs.*"

She takes a forced, deep breath. "Hi." She answers the phone and tries to sound both happy and relax.

She annoyingly listens to Andrew rant on about how awful his day was and how upset he is that his wife and children aren't home to greet him. When he takes a break to breathe, Elizabeth boldly interrupts him.

"Excuse me but do you remember my day? Someone made a threat against your children and you refused to come home and help us. Thanks for that." She doesn't wait for him to respond back. "We'll come home in a little while. They're having fun at the park." She quickly ends the call.

She tips her head back and looks up at the cloudy sky. She squeezes her eyes tightly shut. Thinking of her wedding day no longer fills her with happy emotions; rather dread and guilt. Just months after the best day of her life, Elizabeth experienced the worst day of her life. It was the first time Andrew ever raised his hand to her. Her world seemingly collapsed around her. The sincere, happy-go-lucky, young woman disappeared the moment her body crumpled to the floor with that blow.

She shutters, picks her head up and quickly spans the playground for her children. When she locates them still over by the slides, she walks over to them. It took a minute or two to get their attention. "Hey, girls. We need to be heading home." When they seem unimpressed, Elizabeth continues, "Daddy is home and wants to see you. We need to go."

They both moan but, luckily for Elizabeth, they stop playing and head towards their mother. She patiently waits as their toddler legs slowly take them to her. She gives each of them a quick kiss on the head. "Thank you, girls, for listening so well. Let's get into the car."

The family reluctantly climbs back into the family car and heads home. Elizabeth nervously pulls into the driveway. Andrew's SUV sits in the open garage. She tries to act cheery for the sake of the girls.

"Look! Daddy's home!"

She looks into the rearview mirror at their expression. Neither girl is smiling. They are both staring out the window, emotionless.

GEORGE

George leans over to his beautiful wife and gives her a quick kiss on her cheek. A few camera flashes jump in front of his eyes, nearly blinding him, but he hardly notices. In front of him is everyone he loves. They're smiling and staring back at the happy couple. He looks down at the large cake in front of him. It reads, "Happy 50th Anniversary."

Over the last several weeks, their plans have had to significantly change. Bethany has not moved out and her young kids run the house. She still doesn't have a job which has stressed George financially. He tries to put the stress aside so he can enjoy the rest of the day. He poses with Ethel for a couple more pictures. He climbs to his feet. His legs ache, his head aches, and his stomach is in knots with stress. He plasters on a genuine smile and moves out of the way so Ethel can cut the beautiful cake. The lack of sleep has hit him pretty hard. At least the party is a break from all of the mayhem. He tries desperately to enjoy himself but right after cake, he finds himself getting tired. He sits back in his favorite recliner and shuts his eyes.

"Ugh!"

He moans as a tiny person jumps on his legs and stomach. He opens his eyes and stares around, trying to regain his composure. Sitting on his lap is the oldest of Bethany's children. He stares up at George with innocent eyes.

"Hey, bud. Where is everyone?" George notices the living room is both quiet and empty. He glances down at his gold watch. "Oh my, it is late!" He gently gets to his feet so as not to toss the child to the ground. He stretches his aching muscles. Not surprisingly, several large cracks escape. He looks down and Max is still staring at him. "Are you hungry? Would you like some dinner?"

Max nods then runs to the kitchen. A bit confused over where everyone in his family could be, he follows Max to the kitchen. He watches as Max sprints to the closest chair and plops down. George chuckles.

"Can I have cake for dinner?"

George considers it. At least Max would be quiet for awhile. "Why don't we have some of chicken and mashed potatoes first. If you eat those, then you can have some cake."

"Oh, Grandpa. Please?"

Hearing the pleading tone of voice, George smiles. "Max, is that a good and decent, dinner?"

"Can I have mac and cheese, please?" Max calmly counters.

"You got it, bud."

George turns around to the fridge. He digs around until he locates the already-prepared macaroni and cheese and an opened container of green beans. Before he has time to finish warming up the plate of food, Ethel arrives in the kitchen. He instantly notices the exhaustion on her face. He walks over and puts his arms around her. He can feel her begin to relax. They continue to stand there holding one another until the buzzer of the microwave echoes in the kitchen. George pulls away and grabs the now hot plate. He sits it down next to Max. He returns to Ethel and grabs her hand.

"Where are the rest of the kids? Bethany have them?"

"No, she left about an hour ago. The boys are running around in the backyard and Anna is playing with her dolls on the back deck. "

When Max hears about the fun outside, he jumps off the chair, and skips away.

"Are you done eating?" George shouts. He doesn't hear a response. "Max?" He looks frustratingly at Ethel. She's laughing. He chuckles in hopes of lightening his mood. It doesn't help and he finds himself grumbling aloud as he throws away a full plate of food. As he walks passed Ethel, he plants a quick kiss on her cheek. By the time he arrives at the back door, Max has joined his brothers in the yard. He grabs a nearby chair and pulls it up close to Anna. "What are you doing, sweetheart?"

Anna doesn't look up from her pile of dolls but quietly answers. "Playing dolls, Papa."

George smiles at the little girl. Over the past few weeks, George has proudly watched her go from a destructive and out of control 5 year old to one of respect and responsibility. He rolls his eyes when his glance switches to the boys. They are currently wrestling with one another. As soon as one falls to the ground, the other pounces on him and throws dirt in his face.

"Here."

George looks down next to him. Anna is looking at him and holding up one of her favorite dolls. He takes the tiny doll from her and holds it. She smiles in return. Then she returns to her own play. George leans back in his chair, lovingly setting the doll on his lap. He watches the boys run around the yard until the sun goes down. When it becomes too difficult to see the three tiny shapes, George calls them all inside. Although whining and grumbling respond to George, they all unhappily trek into the house.

"Hey, honey." He patiently waits for his wife to arrive into the kitchen. "Do you think you can help me get them ready for bed? They're a mess."

"Sure," she says. Then she takes a look at the kids. George watches as she smiles and shakes her head. Instantly, George feels calmer. The stress of dealing with all four rambunctious children melts away when he sees her relaxed nature. Ethel corrals the children into the bathroom and George follows behind. The duo helps the children strip off their muddy, wet, clothes down to their underwear. When that nearly impossible task has been completed, Ethel begins bath time for the boys.

After promising George multiple times she's okay, George leads Anna out of the bathroom and down the hall to the back bedroom. Anna races over to the make-shift toy box and begins digging around until she locates two small race cars. She skips over to him and hands him a bright yellow one.

"You want to play cars?" George asks, shocked.

Anna nods. George slowly gets to his knees then brings himself to a sitting position. He laughs as they both take turns mimicking car sounds and crashing into one another. In the other room down the hall, George can hear Ethel struggling to clean the boys. Feeling a little guilty, George continues ramming cars into each other and laughing hysterically at Anna's reaction. After some time has passed, two half-dressed boys with soaking wet hair, dash out of the bathroom. They're laughing and shoving each other. George searches for the remaining strength to get to his feet. His legs are shaking and he becomes nervous to take a step for fear of falling. He takes a deep breath and wills his legs to remain standing. He slides his feet back and forth a few times and manages to make it to the hallway. Anna is only a half-step behind him. He can feel her hand on his belt, seemingly helping him finish the trek to the bathroom. He uses the wall as a guide to make his way to the bathroom. After what seems like an eternity, he makes it to the doorway. He peers inside, not sure what to expect. Ethel is still struggling to dress a very feisty Benji.

"Benjamin Marcus, how come you're not dressed yet? Your sister needs a turn in the tub. Hurry up."

Benji takes one look at George then back at Ethel. He stops whipping his hands from side to side. He, instead, drops them to his side and waits patiently while Ethel helps pull his t-shirt over his head.

"Momma!"

George whips his head around toward the sound. Although he cannot see more than the hallway, a wave of relief flows over him. He stumbles into the living room. Bethany is standing in the middle of the living room, texting on her phone. Her children are crowded around her, squealing and jumping up for attention.

"Bethany, can you please give Anna a bath?"

She doesn't answer. Her nose is still buried deep into her phone.

"Bethany!" George shouts. His frustration is mounting. "Anna needs a bath!" he shouts.

Bethany slowly looks up from her phone. "What? She needs a bath? Can you guys do it? I'm just about to head out."

George can feel his cheeks getting hot. He tries to remain calm in front of the children. They are all looking at him, wondering what he's going to say.

Thankfully, Ethel intervenes. "No, Bethany. You need to stay here. If you want to go out after they're sleeping, that's fine. We're too tired and too old to be taking care of your four children."

"Mom!"

George doesn't wait for Bethany to respond. "No, we are done for the night. Stay here. If you leave, don't come back."

Awkward silence. George glares laser-eyed at Bethany, challenging her. He roughly crosses his arms. Finally, after what seems like an eternity, Bethany begins walking towards the bathroom. George hears the water run in the tub down the hall. He begins to fill with relief.

"Alright, sweetheart. Your turn. Go get a quick bath." He smiles at Anna. His heart softens for a moment when she gives him a huge smile back. He watches her scamper away. He takes a deep breath.

He staggers toward Ethel but then feels his legs give way. He throws out his hands trying to grasp for anything to keep him upright. Failing, he crashes to the carpet.

"Ow!"

"George!"

He allows himself several moments to get himself together before opening his eyes. His vision is blurry and he waits until he can see before attempting to sit up. By this time, both Bethany and Ethel are at his side, pulling him to his feet. Feeling dizzy and shaky, he stands up. No one says a word. Feeling awkward, George staggers to the closest chair. He loses his breath after only a few steps but reaches the chair and collapses.

"Honey?"

He can hear the worry in his wife's voice but he has no more energy to respond. He lifts his head up and looks into her eyes. She walks over and kisses him on the forehead.

"Momma!"

Anna suddenly yells from the bathroom, reminding everyone where she is. Without another word, both Ethel and Bethany leave the room to tend to the unattended children. George tries to relax but panic has long set in. Tumbling to the ground has shaken him. He sits in the chair, trying to calm his racing heart. He clenches his teeth together and squeezes his eyes shut. Finally, relaxation creeps up and he falls asleep.

CAMERON

"How was school today, bud?" Cameron sits in his usual seat at the head of the dinner table. He stares at his ever-quiet son. Although Cam doesn't expect an answer at this point, he keeps pressing forward. "I think you had art class today, right? Did you get to paint anything today?"

CJ doesn't look up from his plate.

"I handed you CJ's picture."

Claire's head is down but Cam can see she isn't eating. "Thanks, Claire," Cam says sarcastically. Cam reverts his attention back to CJ. "It was a beautiful day today. Did you get a chance to go outside?"

Although CJ doesn't respond, Cam perks up a little when their eyes meet for a moment.

"I need a vacation."

Cameron's attention is again broken from his son. His gaze falls to his wife. He scratches his head. "Ok, well, we don't have the money right now."

"Cam, I need a vacation." Cam can hear her tone grow louder and more aggressive.

"Claire!" Cam can't help but shout at her. Realizing his anger is building, he takes several deep breaths before continuing. "We don't have the money right now. You know this. We can talk about this later."

Claire remains quiet. What is left of dinner is finished in silence. Cam finishes his plate and helps CJ take his plate to the kitchen. CJ gently places his plate into the sink and scampers down the hall toward his room. Cam hears CJ's bedroom light turn on and his door quickly shut. Disappointed yet again at CJ's lack of communication, he sets his son's cup and silverware into the sink. He turns to face the refrigerator. He smiles. Front and center is a newly painted picture. Nine perfectly round balls are dancing around a large, yellow sphere on a backdrop of black. Down in the far corner is scribbled 'CJ."

He walks back into the dining room to find Claire still sitting in her seat. He pauses for a moment and contemplates whether to begin the conversation.

"Want to talk?" Cam asks, unsure of what answer he's hoping to hear.

Claire puts her head in her hands but doesn't respond. Her plate has long been cleared of any remnants of food but she still refuses to leave the table. Having become accustomed to Claire's silent pity parties, Cam is unable to find any amount of patience for his wife. He turns around and heads to his bedroom He quickly changes out of his work attire and into a t-shirt and sweat pants. He throws himself onto his bed, wondering if he has the energy to read the book he started the night before. He sits himself up against the wooden headboard with several over-sized pillows. He takes a deep breath and reaches for the book in his nightstand. When he sees the drawer is empty, he quizzically looks around. Then he remembers the night before. The terrible fight he had with Claire comes flooding back to him.

"I need you home more," Claire had said.

"Have you thought that maybe I don't want to be home more?" Cam remembers shouting back.

Sigh.

He throws himself back onto the pillows and looks up at the ceiling in frustration. He puts his hands on top of his head. "Ugh," he moans loudly. He remembers Claire having thrown his book at him. It missed striking him and instead sailed into the open closet. When she failed to hit her intended target, Claire had picked up the remote and chucked it at him as well.

He unhappily climbs out of bed and walks over to the large closet door. He opens it and on the floor, in the corner, is his tattered book. He bends down to pick it up and something catches his eye. It's a gym bag. It's shoved back into the corner of the closet. He reaches over and plucks it out. Although Claire does go to the gym on a regular basis, this is not the bag he recognizes. He thinks for a minute about putting it back and pretending he never saw it. He quickly changes his mind. He grabs it, and carries it back to his bed. He unzips it, careful not to make too much noise to alert Claire. He takes a deep, nervous, breath and reaches inside. The bag does not contain the workout clothes he is expecting. The bag, however, does contain several long, formal dresses, and two, small glittery, clutches. Underneath the clothing is a white envelope. When Cam peeks inside, a stash of Benjamin Franklins stare back at him. He counts and recounts the hundred dollar bills, wondering where she got so much cash. More confusingly, why would she hide it?

A noise from behind him makes him spin around. Claire is standing in the doorway. The pair stand still and stare for several long moments. Cam stares into her eyes while she stares at the bag on the bed. Claire is the first to break the gaze. This breaks the trance Cam is in and he grabs the bag off the bed. He storms up to her and thrusts the bag at her feet.

"Claire! What is this?"

"It's a bag."

Cam opens his eyes wide. "A bag?! I see it's a bag! What is it doing in our closet?"

"I don't know."

"This time that answer isn't good enough. What are yo' doing with all of this money?"

Without saying another word, Cam watches as Claire spins around and walks away. He can hear the front door open then shut rather roughly. Cam chooses not to follow her. He kicks the bag as hard as he can. It slams into the wall in the hallway. He turns around and jumps back into bed. He reaches for the remote to the TV. His hand brushes the wooden picture frame. He picks it up and stares sadly at it. The words "I belong with you, you belong with me" stare back at him. A happy Claire is smiling and Cam is standing behind her with his hands around her waist. He's kissing her cheek. He lays it back on the table but he places it face down. He grabs the remote and clicks it on to his favorite sports channel. He settles himself down, completely abandoning the book idea. He tries to focus on the TV but with his stress level rising, he finds it impossible.

He turns off the television and changes out of his sweat pants and into a nice shirt and jeans. He quickly exits the house and drives the short distance to his favorite bar. He pulls into the closest parking spot. He slams the door shut just as a loud roar of thunder rolls overhead. He walks into the small bar, not sure of what to expect at this time of night. It is busy. He finds a seat at the bar and quickly orders a bottled beer. He looks around but doesn't recognize any-one. Probably a good thing, he thinks to himself. He quickly drinks first beer and orders another one. This one he chooses to drink a little slower. When he has only a few gulps left, he's startled by a heavy smack on the back. He almost chokes on his beer.

"Hey, bud!"

Cameron turns around and sees a large, poorly dressed 30-something-year old man standing behind him. "Hey," Cam responds back, a little confused by the intrusion. When neither man speaks for a few seconds, Cam takes the initiative. "Do I know you?"

"Nope," the man responds. He doesn't move toward or away from Cam but sips at his tall glass of dark beer. "My name is Mark but my friends call me for a good time."

When Mark leans in closer to Cam, Cam can smell the strong scent of alcohol on his breath. Cam turns back around to face the bar. When the bartender makes eye contact with him, Cam signals for another drink. He quickly swallows what is left in his bottle and slams it down onto the bar.

"So, you here by yourself."

The question is loudly posed and startles Cam. He whips around to see the same tall man standing behind him. Now finding himself annoyed by the situation, he turns around.

"Yes, I'm here by myself and I'd like to keep it that way." Cam has to nearly shout to be heard over the now blaring music.

The man takes a seat on the newly vacant stool next to him. "Oh, no way. No one wants to be by themselves. How 'bout I keep you company for a little while."

"No, that's alright. I really just came here to clear my head. I really don't want any company. Seriously," he adds when the man continues to smile at Cam.

Cam rolls his eyes and faces the bar. He tries to ignore the man as he begins to chatter about nonsense. After more than ten minutes, his phone both rings and vibrates in his pocket. He pulls it out, thankful to use it as an excuse to ignore the man further. When he looks down, he sees it's Claire. Disappointed, he turns off the ringer and decides to ignore the call. After a few short rings, the phone is silent. He sets the phone down in front of him and stares at it.

"Oh, Claire," he can't help but say aloud. His brain races to past events again. What am I supposed to do? He thinks to himself desperately. Back when they were first married, everything was perfect. He had started his new practice and was very successful. He had lots of patients and his staff adored him. He worked a lot but Claire was by his side, supporting him through everything. She understood his busy schedule so she kept up the house, took care of all of CJ's needs, including homework and doctor visits, and had dinner on the table waiting for him, no matter what time he arrived home. Even with so much on her plate, she still made time to take care of her ailing mother. In a matter of a few short years, everything changed. He still works long hours but Claire's support has diminished. She no longer keeps up with the daily house work and dinner is rarely made for him. At times, Claire barely gets CJ to his therapy sessions on time. She seems preoccupied by other things.

His thoughts are interrupted again by his vibrating phone. He glances down at the front of the phone. The caller ID reads '*Claire.*'

"Ugh," he says aloud. He anxiously waits for her to hang up. When she finally does, Cam breathes a sigh of relief. However, the relief is quickly dashed when she immediately calls back. "Seriously?" he shouts. His neighbor begins questioning him but Cam ignores it completely. He slams his beer bottle on the bar, startling everyone around him. He chugs the rest of his beer and throws money onto the bar before climbing to his feet and leaving. He doesn't pay attention to the stranger he abandoned but he can hear the man shouting at his retreating back. As soon as he gets outside, he tries to answer the phone but enough time has gone by and she has hung up again. He wonders whether or not to call back. He doesn't need much time to think because his phone rings again. He doesn't allow it to ring one full ring before he answers.

"What?!" he says rudely.

As he listens to the voice on the other end, he can feel the color drain from his face. He becomes sick to his stomach. He doesn't give Claire a chance to finish her sentence before he quickly hangs up.

In a fog, Cam dashes to his car and jumps in. His first thought is to get home as fast as he can. He can't stop his mind from thinking of every negative possibility. As he nears his house, the panic begins to increase twofold. He pulls onto his street and bright lights catch his eye. As he nears them, he realizes the street is littered with people, police cars, fire trucks, and a single ambulance. He throws the car into park as he approaches and leaps out. He sprints to the center of the group of people and looks up.

His entire house is engulfed in flames.

He stands here watching firemen try to get the flames under control. He looks around for his family and a sickening thought occurs to him. Right after Claire left the house, he left as well; leaving CJ by himself.

"Oh no. Oh God, no!" he shouts. He begins running around, desperately looking for his broken family. All of his ill-feelings for Claire disappear at the thought that she or CJ might be seriously hurt. When he doesn't find them, he locates his next door neighbor. He doesn't have to say a word, the woman answers his internal questions.

"Everyone is fine. They are standing over there." She points to the left. Cam jerks his head in the direction where she is pointing. Near one of the police cars, Cam spots the back of Claire's head. He takes off running in that direction. Before he reaches them, she spins around to face him. He can tell she'd been crying. His heart breaks. Although no tears are currently running down her face, her usually flaw-less make up is smudged under her eyes. The intensity of the blaze lights up her face—he can see the tears glistens in her eyes. Cam looks passed her and sees CJ sitting in the back of the squad.

"Is he okay?" Cam asks, beginning to panic again.

Claire nods her head and say, "Yes, no thanks to you."

Cam instantly steps toward her and throws his arms around her. Although she doesn't return the hug, Cam is relieved when she doesn't pull away either. She begins to cry. "Why did you leave him by himself? You know he can't take care of himself."

Cam doesn't answer initially. When he does, he chooses his words carefully. "I was upset and wasn't thinking. I'm sorry." He doesn't let her go. "Are you okay?"

She doesn't answer but he can feel her nod against his shoulder. He squeezes her tighter. After another minute, she pulls herself free. Cam lets her go and instead walks over to CJ.

"Hey, bud. How're you doing?" CJ continues to sit in silence. Cam looks over to the paramedic. When the short man doesn't respond, Cam poses his question directly to him. "Is he ok?"

Strangely startled by being acknowledged by Cam, the man quickly responds, "O-oh, yes. He has a scraped knee and a small bump on his head but otherwise he's fine."

Cam turns his attention back to his son. He grabs his hand. "Did you fall down? What happened?"

From behind him, Claire responds to his question this time. "When the police got here, they found him sitting in the street. He was holding a lighter and a book of matches."

The sick feeling Cam originally felt has not only returned but intensified. He turns back to face his son. CJ has his hands in between his legs, his head is down staring intently at his toes, and not making any eye contact with anyone. Cam steps even closer to his son.

"CJ." When CJ fails to respond again, Cam speaks louder. "CJ, look at me."

CJ doesn't respond. Cam reaches out and touches his son's leg. "CJ…" Cam says, this time no louder than a whisper. He drops his hand to his side. Tears well up in his eyes and he doesn't try to stop them from falling down his face. He walks over to the curb and throws himself down. How did everything get so out of hand, he thinks as the fire behind him rages on; destroying the last of the happy memories his family had.

MARK

Mark wakes up in a hazy fog. He rubs his eyes, trying to focus. After a minute or two, he realizes he's lying in a field; a corn field to be more exact. He looks down at himself. He's wet and covered in both blood and mud.

"Ugh," he mumbles under his breath when he notices he's peed himself. "Disgusting."

He stands up and looks around. The field is enormous. Shin-high corn stalks litter the ground and the only thing in sight is a large, boarded-up barn far off in the distance. His head is pounding. He rubs his temples, trying to alleviate some of the pain; to no avail. The bright sun beating down on him causes him to squint and shield his eyes. He starts walking toward the barn, unsure of exactly where to go. How did I get here? Where is everyone? Why do I have such a horrible headache? When it dawns on him that has no cut or scrape, he wonders whose blood is on his shirt. These and many other questions race through his mind over and over again. He reaches into the back pockets of his dirty, torn jeans. This is where he usually keeps his cell phone. Thank God, he thinks to himself, as he pulls out his now very beat-up phone. As he's flipping through his phone book, the phone rings. It's an unknown number.

Furious at his situation, he rudely answers the phone. "What?"

"Where you at?" a female voice responds.

Mark looks around, trying to see anything he recognizes. Unfortunately, he comes up empty. "I have no idea. Who is this?"

"It's Meagan, dummy," Meagan says quickly.

Mark racks his brain, trying to think of who Meagan is. Then it dawns on him. "Tom's Meagan?"

There is a short pause. "Ummm ... yeah," she says a little uncomfortably. "Where are you?"

"I just said, I don't know!" Mark yells into the phone.

There is another pause. "Listen, how can I come get you if I don't know where to go?"

"Good question, idiot."

"Look around," she says impatiently. "What kind of room are you in? Look outside, what does the neighborhood look like?" When Mark doesn't initially answer, Meagan continues. "I don't have all day. Get a move on."

"I'm already outside. Ok, well, forget it. I'll figure it out." Mark shuts his phone, hanging up on Meagan. With no specific plan in mind, Mark continues his trek toward the barn. As he walks, he looks around, trying to recognize anything. The sun is high and there's not a cloud in the sky.

After he walks for some time, he finally arrives at the front of the barn. The dark brown paint is chipping and falling off. He tries to look through a window to see inside but the level of dirt prevents it. As he ponders whether or not to go inside, his phone rings again. This time, however, it is his mother. He rolls his eyes and screams, "Oh, my God!" He decides to not answer her call. Silencing the ring, he walks around to the other side of the barn. He tries again to recognize his surroundings but still falls short.

What happened? He wonders. He tries to think back to what occurred the night before. He can't remember much more than meeting up with Tom at his house. He scratches his head, completely bewildered. He decides to take a look inside the barn. Maybe there is a tractor or something he can use to get out of here faster. He slowly opens the door. It creaks and moans loudly. He takes a slow, tedious step inside and is overwhelmed by the darkness. Although he could see several windows, dust, grime, and cobwebs cover every one. The light filters in through the now opened door. He looks around, trying to find anything he can use but even though the shadows, nothing is recognizable. He wanders around the room, careful not to trip on anything. Small rodents scamper passed him as he goes deeper and deeper into the secluded barn. From behind him, a loud creak sends him spinning backwards. He doesn't see anything. He turns back around and takes one more step in. The barn door slams shut.

Although he doesn't want to admit it, his heart begins to race. He holds his breath and listens. He decides to leave the barn even though he doesn't get a chance to find anything he can use. He takes a couple small steps toward the door but trips on something small and hard. He tumbles to the ground. He throws his hands out in front of him in an attempt to cushion his fall. Sharp pain shoots through his left hand and another pain radiates up and down his left leg.

He lets out a series of expletives that would embarrass the surliest of bums. He slowly gets to his feet and carefully and slowly walks to the front of the barn. He runs his hand over the door, trying to locate the handle. When he finds it, he throws it open. Before his eyes can adjust to the sudden brightness, something hard hits his cheek with such force, it knocks him to the ground.

"Ow!" he shouts as his left hand hits the ground. Unsure of whether to look at his hand first or the person standing in front of him, he lays on the ground without moving.

A very deep voice slowly says, "Get out of my barn."

"Dude, are you crazy? What's wrong with you? I'm trying to get out of your barn!" Mark sits up completely. He glances down at his hand. Blood begins to drip down his hand. He looks in horror when he sees a rusty nail sticking out of his palm. He groans as he yanks it out. "You are going to pay for this."

"I doubt that," the voice says.

Mark gets to his feet and lunges at the stranger. He misses when the stranger easily steps aside. Mark falls back down to the ground. This time, though, he's careful not to land on his injured hand. He doesn't hesitate to jump back to his feet. He stands there trying to intimidate his aggressor with his body language.

"I am not going to tell you again. Get. Off. My. Property."

Mark continues to stand without moving. He stares at the older, smaller, white-haired man. He puffs out his chest and looks the man in his eyes. The older man wastes no time in taking two confident steps toward the intruder. He raises his hand again to strike Mark. Mark stumbles back. Without another thought, he takes off running far away from the man and his barn. He follows a road up ahead.

Once the barn is no longer visible, he slows his run to a walk. After more than half an hour passes, he runs into the first familiar sight. His dark, forest green jeep gleams in the sun. The front of the car is completely smashed in. All of the windows are broken and some of the glass lies on the ground next to the car. He notices the car is leaning to one side. Walking around to the other side, both tires on the right side are shredded. He laughs to himself. What happened last night? He wonders again.

"Strange," he mumbles to himself. He walks back around to the driver side of the car and pries the door open. He brushes some of the glass on the seat to the ground. Then something catches his eye. A large, plastic shopping bag is stuffed underneath the passenger seat. With shaking hands, he reaches over and snatches it. Inside the bag are bottles and bottles of prescription medications. He looks quizzically through the bottles. Smiling, he grabs a bottle, opens it, and pops several white tablets into his mouth. He jams the bottle into his pocket. After struggling for a minute to swallow the large tablets, he continues searching through the bag. At the bottom, something black and shiny causes him to pause. A brief second or two passes. Making sure he is alone, he grabs the gun. He shoves it in the waist band of his pants. He throws the significantly lighter bag onto the floor of the jeep and he continues up the dirt road. After a few minutes, the dirt road ends and a paved one takes its place. Once on the paved street, he withdraws his cell phone from his pocket. He quickly punches in his friend's phone number and waits for him to pick up.

"Where are you?" Tom says angrily.

"I don't know. I'm standing on a road. Why did I just find my car all smashed up? I thought you drove us out last night?"

"You don't remember?"

Mark waited impatiently for Tom to continue. When silence is his only answer, Mark responds. "Ok, so I don't remember. What happened?"

Tom chuckles. "We met up with Allen. We wanted to use your car to go to the drug store so we went back to your house and got the jeep."

The night's events begin flooding in. Mark thought for a moment. He remembers driving his jeep to a small, remote drug store with Tom and Allen in the car. He recalls pointing the gun at the woman standing in front of the register. Allen grabbed the bag from the woman's trembling hands and they all raced back to the car. They jumped in the jeep and sped away. After that, his memory begins to fade again. There's still no explanation to his wrecked car.

"So, what happened to my car?" Mark asks Tom.

"No idea. You dropped us off at my house because you said you needed to go somewhere. You didn't say where."

"Hmmm. Come get me."

"I don't know where you are."

"Oh yeah. Let me figure it out and I'll call you back."

He hangs up the phone and keeps walking.

Beep. Beep.

He turns around. A large, red pick-up truck is coming toward him. Mark turns around to face them, waving his hand to try to stop the truck. He continues standing in the middle of the road. Finally, the truck slows down. As it pulls up next to him, he sees it contains several teenage boys. Their music is blaring and they are all laughing and cracking jokes. When the truck comes to a complete stop, Mark approaches the passenger window.

"Hey guys. What's going on?"

"Nothing much, you have yourself a little accident?" The driver's eyes divert to the wet spot on Mark's pants. The boys break out into laughter.

"Haha," Mark laughs sarcastically. "Can I get a ride somewhere or not?"

"Oh sure, as long as you don't pee in my truck," the drivers says, still laughing. "Where are you headed?"

"I don't really know, actually. I'm kind of lost."

"Alright, well get in and we'll take you to the gas station."

They open the passenger side door and slide over to the far side. Mark jogs around to the other side and climbs in. He slams the door shut and the truck pulls away.

"So, what's your name, chief?" one of the passengers asks.

Without a second thought, Mark blurts out, "John."

"Well, JOHN," he over emphasizes. "What brings ya out here? You're kinda out in the middle of nowhere." The driver poses the question while eyeing his new passenger.

Before answering the question, Mark asks his own question. "Who are you?"

The driver becomes uncomfortable with the blunt question. "Gavin, I'm Gavin."

Trying to keep the upper hand with the teenagers, Mark continues his own line of questioning, "So, who are you guys?"

The others all introduce themselves. Afterwards, no one speaks. Although the music is still blaring loudly, there is an odd silence within the truck. Finally, in the distance, Mark sees a small, deserted-looking gas station. Although he still doesn't recognize the area, it is still calming to see something more than trees. They pull into the small parking lot. The truck bounces over the many potholes. They pull up next to the only fuel pump. Gavin turns to face their hitchhiker.

"I know the guy that works here. He has a phone you can use."

"Hey, thanks a lot for the ride." Mark climbs out of the truck and everyone but Gavin follow. Mark walks toward the store. He can feel the eyes of the people behind him. He tries to play it off cool. He lumbers into the store and quickly locates the manager. *Manny*, the name tag says, is sweeping the floor near the back of the store.

"Excuse me. Hi. Do you have a phone I can use?" Mark stands upright with his shoulders back, chest out, chin up, and a small smirk on his face. He does make sure his own cell phone is completely tucked away in his pocket; out of sight.

"Why certainly, young man. Come this way."

As soon as the man turns around, Mark rolls his eyes. He follows him back to the register. The manager hands him a black, cordless phone. Mark does not thank him. He takes the phone from his hand and turns away from him. He pretends to dial a number. Faking a phone call is a lot harder than it is in the movies, he chuckles to himself. He waits until Manny has checked out several customers and the store is empty once again.

"All finished?" Manny asks once Mark approaches him with the phone.

"Yep, thanks, man. Hey, can you do me another favor?"

With no hesitation, Manny agrees.

Mark takes a deep breath, and proceeds. "I need some cash." The confused look on Manny's face is what Mark expected to see. "Do you know what cash is?" he continues to berate the gentle, soft spoken, man.

"Well...of course I..."

"Great. I need some." As Mark finishes his statement, he lays the gun from his waistband onto the counter. Manny stares back at Mark, flabbergasted. "3 seconds," Mark continues when he sees the hesitation.

He impatiently waits for Manny to open the register. He sees the man hesitate then reach under the opened drawer. Mark picks up the gun, reaches over and grabs Manny's collar. He hits him in the face with the butt of the gun. Manny falls to the ground. Mark reaches over to the open register and plucks out as much money as he can grab. He sprints out before anyone can walk in. He runs to the red truck and jumps into the driver seat, and pulls away.

PART III

ELIZABETH

She slowly sips her hot tea on the deck. The sun is just beginning to dip down behind the tree line in the back of her yard; her favorite time of the day. Some neighboring children are still playing outside, enjoying the summer air.

"Hello?"

Elizabeth snaps back to reality. She takes a deep breath and releases it before getting to her feet. She takes another gulp of her tea and slowly walks inside. Her sliding glass door opens up to her lavish kitchen.

"What?" she asks, somewhat harshly.

"What do you mean 'what?' Your kids are home."

"Ok. You're their father, you are allowed to watch them."

"You're the one who wanted them, not me. Plus, I'm tired and need a shower."

Elizabeth can feel her anger rising dangerously high. She opens her mouth to yell but stops when she sees two little faces staring at her from the doorway. Both are clutching a large, white paper. Their faces have recently acquired a look of both shock and uncertainty. Trying to change the tension-filled atmosphere, Elizabeth plasters on a half-hearted smile. She bends down so she can be eye level with her children.

"Hey, girls! Did you have fun at Grandma's house? What do you guys have?"

Both girls are hesitant to come forward. They look at each other but finally Maria feels brave enough. She steps toward her mother and holds out her tiny hands to show off her art work.

"Maria! Did you do this? I love this!" Elizabeth enthusiastically takes the scribbled art work from her daughter and looks at it. She then gives her a long hug. Once Maddie realizes everything is okay, she comes forward to hand over her picture as well. Elizabeth makes over Maddie's picture too and she sees her daughter beam at the positive acknowledgement. Elizabeth stands back up and walks over to the fridge. She lets the girls pick where to hang up their pictures.

"Hey, since you're over there, want to grab me a beer?"

Elizabeth's improved mood quickly disappears. She tries to remain calm. She continues to hang the beautiful pictures onto the door of their already full fridge door. She contemplates opening the door and retrieving a cold beer for her clearly lazy husband but only thinks about it for a second.

"Get it yourself."

"Excuse me?"

"You heard me."

She quickly gathers the kids and leaves the kitchen. She knows she's about to pay for her boldness and wants the kids out of sight. With one of her feet in the hallway and one foot in the kitchen, a large hand reaches out and grabs her forearm. She tries to shake it loose but fails. "I need a beer."

Elizabeth refuses to make eye contact with him. She is starting to feel more and more frightened. "The girls want to watch cartoons. Let me go. Now."

Andrew doesn't let go. The grip on her arm gets tighter. Thankfully, the twins do not realize their mother has stopped following them and continued walking into the living room. Elizabeth tries again to rip her arm out of his grasp but is not successful. "Andrew…"

Andrew squeezes her arm tighter. The pain in her arm takes her breath away. Once her arm feels as though it may explode, he let's go. He immediately grabs both her shoulders and throws her against the refrigerator. She bounces off, taking the artwork off with her. She lays there stunned by the extreme measure taken over such a small refusal. She forces her shaky arms and legs to work together long enough to get to her knees. She hangs her head down. The submissive response is answered by a swift kick to the abdomen. It knocks the wind out of her, leaving her gasping for air. She falls down onto her stomach with a loud groan. The moment drags on and on. She finally forces herself to climb to her knees again. Andrew reaches over and grabs a handful of her long locks and pulls her to her feet.

"Let's try this again, shall we?" He smiles not only nicely but with the same amount of malice.

Elizabeth glares at Andrew. She is unsure whether or not to be more angry or frightened. She takes one initial step towards the hall and away from the fridge but the sight in front of her stops her. Maria and Maddie stare at her with petrified eyes. She doesn't want them to witness another fight so she retracts her only step forward. Andrew shoves her hard again into the fridge door. For the second time, she falls down to the ground. This time around, however, although the pain in her shoulder is searing, she is now nothing more than angry. Furiously, she uses her remaining strength and thrusts open the door. She is filled with such disappointment when she sees the beer Andrew is seeking is higher up on the shelves. She stands up on her tip-toes and reaches for one of the glass bottles. After several attempts, she snags one and unhappily hands it over to her husband.

He pretends to drink it even though the cap is still tightly twisted on it.

"What am I supposed to do with this? No beer comes out!"

He chucks it so hard back at Elizabeth that she nearly drops it.

"Thanks," Elizabeth says sarcastically. She hurriedly twists it open and shoves it back at him. Although her legs are shaking immensely, she forces herself to remain calm in front of her tiny audience. She throws the bottle cap into the trash can under the sink and follows the girls into the family room. She exhaustedly plops down onto the couch and awaits the arrival of the girls. Once everyone is settled, Elizabeth turns on the brand new television set to the daily requested children's channel. From her place on the couch, she cannot see down the hall and she wonders what Andrew is doing. She wants to go look but if she's caught spying, the punishment would be nothing compared to what happened in the kitchen. She does try to listen for him but the sound of cartoons and the giggles of the kids drown out the chance of hearing anything else. The three girls enjoy about forty minutes of pointing and laughing, jumping up and down, squeals, and bouncing. When another round of jumping has concluded, Elizabeth makes the call that the always dreaded bath time has arrived.

As expected, they both put up quite a fight. When one girl calms down and becomes complacent, the other one would ruin the moment. However, once they are both undressed, Elizabeth leads them into their adjoining bathroom. She quickly gives them a bath, not bothering to let them attempt to wash themselves. Once their bath is over, she quickly dresses them in their favorite princess pajama sets. She reads them several small books and kisses them both good night. As usual, Andrew is nowhere to be found. When they are both settled into bed, Elizabeth partially shuts their bedroom door and enters her own room. Andrew is already sitting in bed, the television turned onto his favorite sports channel, and is busy feverishly texting on his phone. Elizabeth says no words to him. She quickly changes into her own pajamas and crawls into bed next to him. She tries to lay as close to her side of the bed as possible. She can hear him chuckle into his phone but this only angers her more.

"Who are you talking to?" she asks meekly.

Without hesitation, Andrew responds, "None of your business."

Elizabeth rolls over to face him. "Yes, it is my business. Is it that stupid woman from work again?"

"None of your business." Andrew doesn't even look up from his phone, just keeps texting and smiling.

"None of my business? It is my business! Let me see your phone." When there's no answer, she continues. "Now, please."

Elizabeth looks over and Andrew has made no attempt to comply. Elizabeth lunges at him. Andrew drops the phone onto the bed. She grabs it from him and tries to look at it. She doesn't have a chance to make sense of what she's seeing before a large set of hands reach out and grab her. Andrew yanks her off the bed by her hair and throws her up against the wall. She smacks her head roughly against the wall and continues to slide down the wall onto the floor. Andrew walks over to her and picks her up off the floor. Once she gets to her feet, he wraps his hands around her throat. She starts gasping for air. She tries to plead with him to let her go but only musters a few gurgles. Her face turns red as she begins to run out of air. Her lungs feel as though they may explode. She tries to pry his hands off but she cannot. He doesn't say a single word to her. Just as the spots appear in front of her eyes, he lets her go. She crumples to the ground, gasping. She places both of her hands around her sore throat. She can't bring herself to look at him. She looks down at the ground, trying to force herself to calm down. She can hear Andrew walking around their bedroom; first to retrieve his dropped phone then climb back into bed.

Once he settles himself in, Andrew calmly and quietly says, "Come to bed."

Elizabeth feels sick to her stomach. The very last thing she wants to do is to lie next to him. She doesn't initially move.

"I'm not going to repeat myself," he says just as calmly.

Elizabeth forces herself to stand. Her knees are shaking and she is afraid they may give out before she reaches the bed. She looks up at him for the first time in a few minutes. He is sitting in bed, exactly like he was when she came into the room the first time. After what seems like an eternity, her outstretched hands rest on the side of the bed. Surprising even herself at her strength not to collapse, she throws herself onto the bed. She wraps herself up in the blanket and squeezes her eyes shut. She tries to will herself to fall asleep but her heart is still pounding uncontrollably. She can hear him turn off the television set and place his cell phone down on the night stand. Although her eyes are shut, she can tell the room is no longer brightly lit. He rearranges himself on the bed. He rolls over and smacks her butt. It startles her.

"Love you," he whispers.

Elizabeth doesn't respond.

When her alarm goes off the next morning, she barely has the energy to roll over to silence it. The very restless night is already taking its toll on her. She grabs at her clock, trying to quiet the loud buzzing. As she does this, the large mass of her husband groans. Remembering how upset she is at him, she finds it rather easy to get out of bed and away. Despite her lack of sleep, her memory of last night weighs heavily on her. She walks down the spiral staircase and into the kitchen to make a fresh pot of coffee before the girls wake up. A creaky door upstairs tells her someone else is awake. She peeks around the corner of the stairwell. A still sleepy Maria is stumbling around. Her pajama set, a size too big, hangs loosely off her already tiny frame. Her hair is a frazzled mess on top of her head.

"Good morning, sweetheart," she whispers to Maria. "Did you sleep okay?"

The girl doesn't say a word but rubs her sleepy eyes and nods. Elizabeth meets her halfway up the stairs and picks her up. She quietly carries her down the rest of the steps. The pain in her rib cage intensifies with the sudden strain. She walks into the kitchen and plops the child onto the counter. She quickly makes her coffee, knowing if Maria is awake, Maddie is only a few minutes behind. Once the coffee has finished brewing, she grabs her daughter off the counter and places her gently on the floor. She fills her largest coffee cup to the brim. She reaches for Maria's hand and leads her into the living room. She sits on the carpeted floor and turns on some early morning cartoons. She barely has time to get settled when yet another child wanders into the room. She takes a quick sip of her strong coffee then gets to her feet.

"Good morning! Did you sleep alright?" As did her sister, Maddie nods her head but doesn't say anything. She rubs her eyes and gives her mom a hug. "Wanna come watch some cartoons with us?"

Elizabeth smiles at her daughters and walks her to where her sister is already sitting. The three of them sit together for a while watching cartoons and laughing. Fifteen minutes or so pass and Elizabeth hears yet another door open upstairs. She can't help but tense up at the sound. The thoughts of the night before creep into her mind. What a horrible night. She arranges herself so she doesn't have to look at him when he emerges down the stairs. She focuses hard on watching the very childish show. She can, however, hear him enter the kitchen and pour himself some coffee. After what seems like forever, she can hear him walk back upstairs and into their shower. She rolls her eyes even though no one sees it.

"You guys want some breakfast?" She breaks the silence and interrupts their trance on the cartoons. At first no one answers. Finally, a switch goes off in both girls' head and they jump up and start cheering for food as though it is a sporting event. Elizabeth chuckles and climbs to her feet, taking her now empty coffee cup with her. The threesome head back into the kitchen. The smaller girls make themselves comfortable on their little table and chair set. They sit calmly and wait for Elizabeth to come back over with their breakfast. Elizabeth quickly puts together a small plate of yogurt, bananas and blueberries, and a small cup of milk. Trying to balance everything, she slowly brings over the plates and cups. As she sits down the last cup of milk, Andrew walks into the kitchen, dressed to kill as usual.

"I'm going to head out. I have to work late so don't wait up."

Elizabeth can feel her face getting hot. She doesn't make eye contact with him. She debates with herself whether or not to say anything. As he turns to leave, she decides to speak up. "You can't be late tonight. We have a dinner date planned with my brother."

"Elizabeth," Andrew says. She can tell by his tone what is coming next. "I have to work. If you want to keep all your nice things, you'll stop complaining about me working."

Elizabeth explodes with both bottled up rage and frustration. She quickly walks away from the children's table. It takes only a few steps to get in front of Andrew. Before she can stop herself, she places her hands on his chest and shoves him with all her might. He is barely knocked off balance but is still shocked at her reaction. She starts to scream at him but most of what she screams is inaudible. Elizabeth cannot think straight, her frustration clouds any chance of common sense thinking.

She pounds on his chest and tries to spit out a few clear sentences. "You promised me you'd go today! You promised me!!"

Although her back is to her kids, she can hear them begin to whine. This doesn't calm her like it has in the past. Andrew reaches over and grabs both of her wrists. He begins to squeeze them. Elizabeth tries to pull free. She still screams at him as she tugs with all her might to get away from him. After one good tug, Andrew let's go and she falls backward. She falls into the children's plastic table, knocking over the cups and plates onto the floor. Both girls begin to scream. A little dazed, she gets to her feet and wipes away several tears that have appeared. Her hands are shaking and her adrenaline has kicked in.

She tries desperately to calm down but when she can't, she angrily spats, "Just go to work. That's the only thing you're good for anyway."

She turns around and leaves the kitchen. She can feel his eyes on her as she exits. She rushes upstairs to her bedroom and slams the door shut. She paces the large master suite several times before she throws herself onto the bed. She sobs uncontrollably into her pillow. She hears the front door shut just as loudly as she shut her bedroom door. She cries until she falls asleep.

• • •

She slowly opens her eyes about an hour later. Still feeling somewhat in a fog, she stretches and climbs to her feet. Once she's standing, she stretches her back and realizes a pain in her side. She lifts up her shirt and sees a large bruise beginning to form. She rubs her eyes. She then remembers her daughters were left downstairs by themselves. She panics and sprints down the stairs. Miraculously, both girls are sitting on the floor in the family room. When she sees the girls laughing and, more importantly, breathing, she lets out a sigh of relief. They see her but don't initially run to her. They sit there, covered in something red, just staring at her. She smiles at them. When she walks over to them, she can see what they're covered in: spaghetti sauce. She turns around and sees the refrigerator door is ajar. She closes her eyes for a second. First, she thanks God for watching over her kids while she selfishly walked away from them. Then she prays for extra patience to deal with the mess. She walks even closer to them and sees the carpet is also splattered with sauce. It is in their hair, all over their faces, and their pajamas are drenched.

"What did you guys get into? Are you supposed to be in the refrigerator?" Both girls look at each other but then shake their heads no. They are still smiling mischievously. "Alright, let's get cleaned up. Last one to the bathroom is a rotten egg!" Elizabeth laughs as she races to the downstairs bathroom. She can hear them laughing as they race after her. Once in the bathroom, she draws a warm bath. When the girls are settled, she wanders into their bedroom to find another set of clothes to wear. She can hear them splashing and laughing. She digs through the drawers until she finds two pairs of matching outfits. She reenters the bathroom and sees, not surprisingly, her children have made no headway towards getting themselves clean. She grabs the nearest washcloth and begins cleaning them off. She spends the most time getting the tomato chunks out of their hair. After the bath, she dresses them quickly. She watches them scurry away together, giggling and shoving each other. Elizabeth doesn't follow them. She sits down onto the floor. She looks down at her hands. Her soft manicured hands are shaking. She shakes them vigorously in an attempt to calm down but it doesn't work. After closing her eyes and taking several deep breaths, the tightness in her chest is not subsiding. She can hear a loud ruckus down the hall.

"Not now," she mumbles quietly to herself.

She pulls herself up. She stretches her back again and takes two more deep breaths in preparation for another disaster. She takes slow, lingering steps down the carpeted hall until she finally arrives to the girls' play room. She forces herself to look inside. There are toys everywhere. The cabinet that usually contains the plethora of Barbie dolls is now swung wide open. There are pink and purple building blocks stacked into piles; many piles. The tiny television set has fallen off the top of the dresser and is lying on the floor next to them. The girls are huddled close to each other. Elizabeth can barely get through the door to see what they're doing. Then she sees the coloring.

"What are you girls doing?"

They both look up from what they're doing. Elizabeth is expecting to see guilty looks on their faces and is surprised to see only sheer happiness. Maria is the first to get to her feet. She skips over and hands her a beautifully colored pony.

"Oh, this is beautiful!" Elizabeth looks over to where Maddie is sitting. The blue carpet is heavily marked up with several different colored markers. Slightly panicking over how to get that out before Andrew sees it, Elizabeth scratches her head. "Alright, girls, how about we take a break and do a little shopping?"

"Yeah!" They both squeal in unison.

"Let's grab your shoes, then." Elizabeth helps two energetic and rambunctious toddlers into their tennis shoes. This proves to be a bigger challenge than she anticipates. When Maddie has both her shoes on and laced up, Maria runs around and hides. After a small struggle, Elizabeth places both tennis shoes on her tiny feet. Before she can get them laced up, Maddie has already taken off her right shoe. "Alright, never mind." She doesn't bother to lace up Maria's shoes or put Maddie's back on. "Let's just get into the car." She helps the girls crawl into their seats and buckles them in. She quickly throws Maddie's extra shoe onto the floor underneath her and shuts the door. Elizabeth gets into the driver side. When her door shuts, the children begin to chatter loudly amongst themselves. Elizabeth tries to remain calm but it isn't working.

"Girls! Girls! Girls!" The silence finally arrives. "Why don't we just be quiet for a little while." She backs out of the driveway. She pulls out her cell phone and dials the number to her favorite pharmacy. She orders a refill for her anxiety medication. Definitely can't get there fast enough, she thinks to herself. The silence in the backseat is broken by Maddie's loud giggling. Elizabeth presses the gas pedal a little harder, hoping to accelerate her arrival to the pharmacy. She pulls into the stony parking lot. "Thank goodness," she says aloud.

"Goodness." A tiny voice echoes behind her.

Elizabeth chuckles. She jumps out and the sun hits her in the face. She looks up at the sky. It's warm and inviting. She quickly stretches her stiff muscles. She doesn't say another word to either girl but helps them out of their car seats. Neither twin puts up a fight when she finishes putting on and lacing up their shoes. The minute Maria's laced feet hit the stones, she takes off running for the tiny store.

"Maria! Maria! Stop!"

Elizabeth shouts to Maria but Maria acts as though she doesn't hear anything. Elizabeth watches as she continues to run until she gets to the front door. She is, however, unable to open the door. Elizabeth grabs Maddie's hand and they jog over to Maria.

"Maria! What have I told you about taking off running? You could have gotten hit by a car or someone could have come up and taken you. Do not EVER do that again." When Maria doesn't seem to be paying attention, Elizabeth continues, "Maria, did you hear me?"

Maria nods her head.

"Honey, what did I say, then."

Said with some hesitation, Maria says, "Don't run."

"Close enough."

They walk inside. The air conditioning, which is turned up a little too high, causes Elizabeth to shiver. She lets go of Maddie's hand and both girls scurry away. There's only one other person she can see walking around. She walks down the nearest aisle and spots her children looking through the small section of plush, stuffed animals. Elizabeth walks over and grabs each child by the hand.

"Hey, girls. Let's go over here. We can come back over when we're finished."

She tries to lead them away from the toys and toward the pharmacy but it's difficult to break their hold on the fluffy animals. After much prodding, pleading, and a few crackers, the trio head to the back of the tiny store. Maria shakes Elizabeth's hand loose and tries to skip away. Elizabeth is quicker and roughly grabs her arm. She forces her daughter to hold her hand.

"Stay with me."

The family continues to walk to the back of the store where they see a sign reading "pharmacy."

The man working behind the counter looks up and smiles. "Hello! How have you been, Elizabeth?"

"Oh, pretty good," Elizabeth says more cheerily than she felt. "Busy with the girls."

"We are a little backed up, it'll just be a couple more minutes."

Elizabeth turns around and heads back to the front of the store. She lets go of both girls' hands but reminds them to stay close to her. They laugh and joke with each other but both young kids stay within reach of their mother.

Although she is impatient and cannot imagine walking around this pathetically small store for very long, she desperately needs her meds. After some time has passed, she glances at her cell phone in her pocket. Her prescription should thankfully be ready. As if it could read her thoughts, an overhead speaker clicks on.

"Miller, to the pharmacy at your convenience."

She looks disappointingly in the direction of the pharmacy. She can't help but feel a little angry. She gets Maddie and Maria's attention and gently leads them away from the toys and back towards the pharmacy. She stands next to the pharmacy, hoping to speed things along. She glances over at the pharmacy and sees a young woman she didn't recognize, standing behind the pharmacist. The man is helping a man Elizabeth presumes to be Mr. Miller. The pharmacist is not smiling. Now more intrigued than mad, she continues walking closer. She can see a tiny metal bench sitting adjacent to the counter. She heads in that direction. As she gets nearer, she tries to listen to the conversation but cannot make out a single word.

She watches the pharmacist disappear behind the counter for a minute or two. Then he reemerges with a large bag.

"Momma," a small voice jerks Elizabeth back to reality. She forgets for a moment where she is.

"What, sweetheart." Elizabeth bends down to get eye level with her daughter.

"Momma," Maddie repeats but slightly quieter.

"Yes."

Even quieter yet, Maddie whispers, "I have to go potty."

Elizabeth smiles. "Ok sweetheart. Let me get my medicine and we'll go to the ba…"

Her words are cut off by a loud *pop-popping* sound. Elizabeth immediately stops speaking and snaps to attention. Without another thought, she grabs both girls and throws them behind her. She looks around at the sound of the noise. She glances at Mr. Miller's face for the first time. He shows no emotion as he looks back at her. Her heart is pounding out of her chest. She pulls her glance away from the man to the pharmacist behind the counter. The once lively man is now slumped onto the floor. She feels sick. Maddie begins to cry. This only speeds up Elizabeth's already racing heart. Her hands shake even though she is trying to keep both girls behind her small frame.

"Please…"

She watches the man raise his gun to her. She squeezes her eyes shut, praying this is a horrible dream. She hears the gun go off but knows nothing else.

GEORGE

Today is the day. Years and years of hard work and dedication has led up to this very day. He looks at himself in the mirror. He leans forward. The deep wrinkles around his eyes and mouth and the dark circles pooling under his lower eye lids remind him how old he really is. He quickly combs through the little hair he has remaining. Standing straight up and squaring his shoulders, he smiles.

"Very nice, dear."

George doesn't need to turn around to see the look on Ethel's face. He re-straightens the never worn polka dot bow tie and rearranges his suspenders. He turns around slowly so as not to exacerbate his tender hips. He looks at Ethel, who is sitting on the end of the bed adjacent to him.

"I think I'm ready," he says proudly.

"You look lovely, honey."

George smiles and kisses her. "Thank you. I have everything packed so we can leave early tomorrow."

"Ok," Ethel responds quietly.

George staggers out of the house. Most days the walk to his car is long. The dread that comes with each step slowly intensifies the closer he gets to work. Not today. He finds his step is lighter than usual. George opens the door. Before he gets in, he turns around to face the street. The sun is shining brightly in the sky. Its warmth hits his face and reminds him how perfect the day is going to be. He looks around. The neighborhood is just going on with its usual morning. No one seems to notice this special moment. He allows the breeze to graze his face for another minute before climbing into his car. He sits down and buckles his seat belt around him. Taking in the familiar sights and smells surrounding him, he smiles to himself. He takes one last look around then backs out of the driveway. As he's pulling away, he sees his perfect Ethel, standing on the porch, like she always did, waving at him like she always does.

He pulls away, reminding himself for the tenth time today how lucky he is.

The drive to work is a short one. He pulls in and for the first time in forty years, is no longer filled with dread. He quickly parks and gets out to face the sunshine again. He stretches his achy body, then heads straight to the front door, straightens his posture, lifts his head up, and opens it.

He walks casually in, smiling at a few people he knows. He walks to the break room to clock in. Once he arrives, he sees more than half the staff located around a small table. They all turn to face him when he enters. It catches him off guard and he drops the bag he's carrying.

Seeing the surprised look on his face, the manager shouts "Happy last day, George!" Everyone erupts into applause. George smiles broadly and soaks in the accolade. When it begins to slow, he walks over to the table and sees a white sheet cake and a card signed by everyone. The cake reads, "Welcome to retirement."

"Oh, thank you, everyone. I've very much enjoyed working with all of you."

Several people walk up to him and give him a hug while others shake his hand. After more celebrations, the manager calls an end to the break and the party begins to dissipate. George is one of the few to leave the tiny room. He walks over to the half-eaten cake and takes another piece. He eats it slowly, enjoying the wonderful atmosphere and good cake. He wipes his mouth with a colorfully decorated "Happy Retirement" napkin. He staggers to the front counter and begins gathering the trash and moving the smaller packages to the back office.

"George!"

He turns to the sound of his name.

Scott stands there with his arms crossed. George isn't sure what kind of mood to expect out of him.

"Yes, sir."

"Oh, you don't have to 'sir' me. This is your last day! Tell me what you are going to do with yourself now."

George allows himself to relax a little. "Oh, yes. Ethel and I have been saving for a beach condo for years. We are going to our beach house for a couple of weeks; just the two of us." He thinks about the previous night. Bethany yelled and made a fuss but she is finally out of the house.

"That sounds wonderful. Make sure you don't be too lax today. We still have a business to run."

There it is; the reason for the hello. "Yes, sir."

He walks away from Scott and toward an employee restricted area. He opens the swinging door, trying to remain positive. He sweeps the dusty floor then runs a mop up and down the aisles. No one enters the backroom to distract him so his work goes quickly. Afterwards, he grabs the dust pan and broom and heads outside. This is, by far, his least favorite activity. The parking lot is covered in potholes and crumbled cement. To say it's a safety hazard is putting it mildly. He glances down at his gold watch.

"Ugh."

It is about lunch time and the parking lot is due to fill up. He tries to hurry along but his aching back and painful knees prevent him from moving faster than a turtle. With the sun beating down on him, he has to stop several times to wipe the sweat from his forehead. He finishes sweeping the parking lot and gratefully walks back into the air conditioning.

"George!"

Another voice shouts above the busy entrance. He looks around and sees a familiar face, smiling and waving.

"George!" she shouts again. He begins to walk in her direction. His legs begin to feel weak so he stands where he is. The beautiful woman continues walking towards him. He looks at her hand and sees a bouquet of white carnations and yellow roses. Once he reaches her, they embrace.

"Jane! What are you doing here?"

Jane brushes her graying hair out of her eyes. "Are you serious? I wouldn't miss your last day! How has it been going?"

George smiles at his daughter. You flew all the way here?" he asks in astonishment.

"I did. Here." She hands him the bouquet.

George smells them and the scent brings yet another smile to his face. "I'm so glad you came here. Would you like to come to dinner after work with Ethel and me?"

"Dad, I would love to."

George's stare strays from Jane's eyes to the right of her. Scott stands several yards behind her. He looks down at his watch. His lips are pursed together tightly and the unblinking glare makes George nervous. His stare seems to penetrate into him and George's initial happiness seems to disappear.

"Ok, well I need to get back to work. If you want, you can stay with Ethel until I get off. We can go to dinner at that new fish fry place when I leave. Sound good?"

"Sounds perfect," Jane is still smiling.

They embrace one more time and Jane leaves George standing there holding the flowers. He watches her walk away feeling both happy to see her but angry at the unreasonable glaring from Scott.

As soon as Jane is out of sight, Scott reappears in front of him. "Hey, bud! How is it going?"

George looks suspiciously at Scott. "It's going fine."

"Oh, I was just wondering," Scott says with a strangely big smile on his face. "If you have time to stand around talking to a pretty girl, you don't have enough work to do. When you are done doing nothing, come see me in my office."

George stands in place completely flabbergasted. He watches Scott walk towards his office. He waits until he disappears behind the closed office door before heading back to the tiny break room. He carefully shoves the floral bunch into the already tiny, half full locker and slams the door shut. He considers not going to Scott's office. It's pretty obvious that it wasn't really optional, based on his tone. He sighs loudly. Several people near him, look in his direction. He doesn't make eye contact with them. He keeps his eyes straight ahead and doesn't say another word to anyone. He arrives at the closed office door. He raises his hand to knock but stops himself. There are plenty of things for him to do, he doesn't need to stop by the office. He lowers his hand and is about to turn around. The door opens.

"Hey, George. Come on in. Let's talk about your work today."

George walks in and shuts the door behind him. He takes a seat across from Scott. A large oak brown desk separates the pair. George impatiently waits for Scott to begin the conversation. In the meantime, he looks around, admiring the many plaques on the wall.

"I received those plaques after years and years of hard work."

Scott's harsh voice seemingly echoes in the tiny office. Not sure how to respond to his comment, George remains quiet. He sits up a little straighter and waits for Scott to continue.

"I know this is your last day. I definitely applaud how hard you've worked. Not many people can say they've dedicated themselves to that many years of loyal service. But just because today is your last day doesn't mean you can take the day off."

"But sir, I'm still…" George tries to defend his actions.

"I still have a business to run."

"I know sir, but…"

"Listen, half of your day is over already but why don't you go back out there and act like this is your first day and you have something to prove?"

George is appalled when Scott finishes his speech with a wink. He waits for a moment before climbing to his feet. No other words are exchanged. Feeling more awkward than inspired, he leaves the office. He heads to the front counter and waits on several customers. He looks at his watch and is disappointed when he sees he is nowhere near time to clock out.

He groans.

From behind him, someone clears their throat. George turns around and sees Scott staring at him. He is not smiling. George turns around and makes himself look busy. He waits on several other customers then tidies up the front. Once all of the larger packages are taken to the designated area, he sits down on a chair in the back. He tries to stretch the pain in his back away but it only increases. He stands up and stumbles over to the broom. He slowly pushes the broom around until the clock on the wall reads 5:30. Thankfully, time to leave. He sets the broom aside. Making a bee-line for the break room, he makes no eye contact with anyone. Several people try to get his attention but he ignores them. He clocks out, grabs his few things and walks out the front door. Happily, he sees the sun is still shining. It's warm and lifts his spirits. He takes his time walking to his car, realizing this is the last time he's going to have to make this walk. This makes him sadder than he is expecting. He arrives at his car and just stands there. He turns around and sees Scott is once again staring at him; this time from the front door. George climbs into the car. In a rush to get out of the dreadful parking lot, the tires squeal loudly. He drives onto the main road, feeling truly excited for the first time. He taps his hands on the steering wheel. He runs through the list in his head of everything he needs to pack tomorrow morning. The several weeks spent with Ethel and Ethel alone is going to be the best start to retirement.

He cranks the radio up several more notches and the oldies blast back at him. As he heads farther into town, the traffic starts to increase. He slows down even more. Cars swerve around him. He ignores everything else around him. The only thing flooding his thoughts is his beautiful Ethel.

An object to his right, catches his eye. A small, blue, car is barreling towards him. With his slow reflexes, he pushes down hard onto the brake pedal. He loses control of his boat of a car. He squeezes his eyes shut just as the front end smashes into a telephone pole.

CAMERON

Cameron sits down on the tiny sofa. He glances down at his watch. It's still early in the evening and the tiny apartment is surprisingly quiet. Becoming comfortable in such a small living space has taken some getting used to. Claire is sitting in an adjacent chair, reading. As he stares in her direction, his mind drifts away.

The fire that raged through his home did more than just destroy the material items. His family has become even more fractured. When CJ gets home from school, he rarely leaves his room, Claire spends most of her days in the nursing home with her mother, and Cam loses himself in his work. Only minimal conversation happens now.

"So how is Mary doing today?"

Cam watches Claire take a sip of the red wine. Finally, Claire responds without looking in his direction. "She's the same."

Cameron is unsure of whether to continue the conversation. He breathes in deeply and decides to inquire more. "Well, then how was the doctor's appointment?"

There's a hesitation before she responds. "It went alright. Her tests came back like we expected."

Cam can see the sadness in her eyes. He opens his mouth to offer comforting words but quickly changes his mind. He just doesn't possess the sympathy.

Claire gulps down the rest of her wine. "How was work?" Claire asks, changing the subject.

"It was alright," he lies. "I was pretty busy."

Uncomfortable silence follows. When neither person speaks, Cam watches Claire climb to her feet to refill her glass. "Do you want more?" she asks, noticing his empty glass.

He glances down and thinks for a second. "Nah, I'm good, but thanks."

He watches her disappear into the kitchen. Cameron sits back in his chair, propping his feet up on the coffee table. After a minute, Claire reemerges holding a dangerously full glass in one hand and her brand new cell phone in the other. She sits back down onto the couch, putting her legs underneath her. She leans over and puts her glass on the side table. She begins checking her phone for messages. Cam looks over at her. He gets a sick feeling in the pit of his stomach when he sees a small smile begin to creep into the corner of her mouth. He can't stop himself from speaking out.

"Who's the message from?"

Without batting an eye, she states, "Oh, nobody. It's just someone from work."

Angrily, Cam says, "Well you don't work, so how can that be?"

"Oh, don't be such a jerk. It's someone I used to work with."

"You know I don't believe you. Everything we've been through and you continue to talk to him."

"I'm not talking to him! Do you want to look at my phone? I'm talking to Samantha. Why do you have to do this every time?"

"You know why I do this all the time. You lie all the time, Claire. That's why I don't trust you."

"I'm trying to fix things with us. I've been completely honest with you."

Cam sarcastically chuckles. "Honest? Are you kidding me?"

Claire stands up. "Cameron, you know I've been trying to work with you on things but I can't keep doing it if you're going to accuse me all the time."

"I wouldn't have anything to accuse you of if you'd stop lying."

"What am I lying about now?"

"Last week when I asked you yet again why you had all of that money in your bag, what did you say?"

Claire's tone suddenly quiets down. "I told you, I was planning..."

"...on taking me on a trip for my birthday," Cam interrupts. "Where were we going to go?"

"I hadn't figured that part out yet. Why is it so surprising that I'd want to do something nice for you?"

"Oh, Claire, really? Ok, forget it. Let me see your phone." He outstretches his hand.

Claire hesitates. She glances down at her phone. She looks back up at him and defensively snaps, "I don't need to show you anything."

Cam turns around and quickly walks out of the living room. On his way out, he punches the wall which sends a picture frame crashing down to the ground. Claire stands in the living room, in shock.

Cam stumbles out to his car. He tries to open the door but realizes he forgot his car keys inside. He swears under his breath at his stupidity. He turns back around and reenters the house. He makes a bee line straight for the kitchen where he left his keys. Claire is already in the kitchen, downing yet another glass of wine. She looks at him but doesn't say anything. Cam refuses to make eye contact with her. He grabs his keys and once again heads for the front door.

"Cam!" Claire shouts to his retreating back. Cam pauses for a mere second but doesn't turn around. He continues walking out of the house. He slams the door behind him. He gets into his car and turns on the engine. The radio plays softly. He throws the car into reverse. When he is about half way down the driveway, he sees the front door open. Claire stands on the front porch with her hands tightly crossed, as though she's cold. She makes no attempt to stop him from leaving. Cam peels out onto the road, leaving his wife at the doorstep.

He glances at his watch and notices how late it is. He yawns. He grabs his cell phone and dials the number of his younger brother. After a few rings, the voice of a drunken man answers.

"Hey, bro. What's up?"

"Hey, Corey. I was just wondering what you're doing."

"I'm drinking, of course."

"Can I meet up with you? I could use a drink or two."

"Sure!" Corey says.

After a minute more of talking, Cam gets the location of the local bar. Cam pulls into the rather full parking lot. He drives around looking for a parking spot. He finds one in the very back corner. As he walks into the bar, cigarette smoke smacks him in the face. He coughs twice. Through the haze, he finds his brother surrounded by young, beautiful women. He pushes through the crowd.

"Hey, man, how are you doing?"

Corey turns to face him. Although both of his hands are occupied with beers, Corey throws his arms around Cam's neck. 'Hey, bro! Want a drink?"

"God, yes!" Cam says. "I've had a horrible day."

Corey walks over to the bartender. The young woman smiles flirtatiously back at him.

"My brother, Cammy, over there, needs a beer. He's having a rough day."

"Sure thing," she says and walks to the other side of the bar. She returns to Corey wearing the same smile. "Tell your friend, it's on the house. No one needs to have a bad day; especially the good looking ones."

Corey smiles back at her. He juggles the three beers in his hand and staggers back to his brother. Slightly slurring his words, Corey says, "That cute girl over there says it's free." He slides one of the beers in Cam's direction. "Maybe I should sleep with her for paybacks."

Cam smiles at the comment. Clearly nothing has changed. "So, how's the new job going?" Cameron asks.

"Oh you know," Corey says, "living the dream." After another pause says, "I quit."

Cam rolls his eyes, smiles, and leans back in his seat. He takes a quick gulp of his beer. Not at all surprised by his younger brother's response, he crosses his arms over his chest. "What did Madeline have to say about that? I'm sure she's not very happy about that."

Corey grins. "Nah, she wasn't. Good thing I got rid of her too."

"Oh, Corey. Is it weird that I'm actually disappointed? I really liked her." Cam says. Cameron looks at his brother. Although there is almost five years between them, they can easily pass as twins. Their dark green eyes lock after a moment of awkward silence.

Corey is still grinning. "It happens. How's Claire? Still driving you crazy?"

Cameron wonders just how honest to be. After seconds of deliberation, he responds, "She's fine. I've been working a lot and I don't usually get home until late. She's been spending a lot of time with her mom."

"Are you sure she's always visiting her mother?"

Cameron cannot stop himself from becoming angry. However, he's not exactly sure what is making him so mad. Was it the truth behind his brother's question? Was it the fact that Claire's past actions made him question her honesty? Was he mad at himself for trying to trust her again? He looks down at his drink. He chooses not to answer the question. After a few very quiet moments, Cameron changes the subject. "CJ's birthday party is coming up. Are you coming?"

"Of course, dude." Corey downs the shot of vodka on the table. "Where are you having it since you guys don't have a place anymore."

Cam rolls his eyes at his brother's insensitivity. "We have a house. It's just, well, getting fixed."

"You mean being rebuilt?"

"Shut it," Cam says somewhere between joking and serious. "Anyway, Claire rented a small pavilion. The address is on the invite."

"Can I bring my girlfriend?"

Cam stares quizzically at Corey. "I thought you broke up with her?"

"Oh, little brother, every hoe is replaceable."

"Ugh, of course. Stop calling me little bro. I'm older than you."

"Then why do I always act older?"

"Partying all day and night, quitting your job and moving in with mom is not very mature."

"Who needs to be mature, anyway?"

Cam laughs.

"So, what's the real reason you came out today? I know Claire didn't just let you come out."

"Yeah, she didn't let me. We got into another fight. I know she's still seeing that stupid prick, Lee, from her old job."

"We should go set his car on fire."

The comment takes Cam completely off guard. "Of everything we could do, why do you want to set his car on fire? That's a little harsh, don't you think?"

"Well, no. You've been with her for how many years?"

"12 years. 12 long, long years. I can't believe how fast it's falling apart."

"Well," Corey says, raising one of his beers to the ceiling. "Here's to your crumbling marriage."

"Here's to you not being able to keep anyone," Cam says.

Cam raises his own bottle and both men chug their beers, each toasting to their different failures. Once the beers have been consumed, they slam the bottles onto the bar. Cam waves over the bartender and quickly orders another round.

"Hey!"

Cam hears Corey shout from behind him. He turns around. Corey had gotten off his stool and is standing behind him. Standing next to him is a tall and very beautiful woman. Unable to stop himself, his heart skips a beat.

"Who is this fellow?" she says to Corey, but making eye contact with Cam. Cameron sits up a little straighter and waits for the formal introduction.

"Oh, have you met Cam?" Corey looks over at Cameron and winks. Cam smiles back. He extends his hand and smiles.

"Hey, I'm Cameron. What's your name?"

She smiles back. "Dina."

She places her hand on his arm. Cam is feeling nervous. Wow, she's beautiful, he thinks. His mind goes blank for a moment as for the reason he came out in the first place. He glances down and notices his silver wedding ring. He touches it with his thumb. It feels cold.

"Dina, why don't you let my friend here buy you a drink?"

Dina looks slightly confused. "Friend? I thought you said he was your brother?"

Cam snaps his head to the direction of Corey. "How'd she know we're brothers, Corey?"

When Corey doesn't answer, Cam presses him further. "Corey. Are you trying to fix me up with someone?"

"Technically, I'm not fixing you up with anyone."

"Hey," noticing the increasing tension, Dina interjects. "I'm just getting thirsty. Cameron, why don't you just buy me a drink?" She smiles again at him.

"I...I gotta go, guys. Hey, Corey, I'll see you later."

Cameron gets to his feet without paying his bill at the bar. He quickly exits before anyone can stop him. He gets into his car and just drives around. He drives around until he can't keep his eyes open any longer. Emotional exhaustion takes over and he wills himself to drive the short distance back to their temporary residence. He parks in his usual spot on the side of the road and gets out. He tries to be quiet but the closer he gets to the front door, the angrier he becomes. All of the lights are out throughout the house and the front door is locked. He loudly unlocks and opens the door and shuts it even louder than he intends. He drags himself through the house until he grabs the few essentials he needs to make himself comfortable on the couch. He kicks his shoes off and curls up into a tiny ball. He pulls the fuzzy blanket up to his chin, hoping it would calm him, however it has the opposite effect. The blanket is covered in Claire's favorite perfume. He takes a deep breath in through his nose and he's filled with not only memories but sadness.

When his alarm finally goes off in the morning, he unhappily pulls himself up. He is purposely getting up before Claire so he doesn't have to interact with her. The sun, along with Claire, has not risen yet so he takes advantage of the calmness. He brews a large pot of coffee and packs a lunch bag. When the coffee is finally ready, he grabs his favorite mug, fills it with caffeinated liquid, and sits on the back porch. He looks down at his wardrobe and realizes that all of his work clothes are in his bedroom closet. He racks his brain trying to come up with another solution so he doesn't have to wake up Claire. The mere thought of having a conversation, either positive or negative, with his cheating wife set off any relaxation and calmness he'd acquired for the past forty minutes.

He pours the remaining coffee from the mug into a travel mug and adds fresh coffee on top. He straightens out the wrinkled clothes he slept in and walks out the front door. He makes sure to lock the door behind him. He gets back in his car and hesitates. He looks up at the window that connects the outside world with Claire. Peering through the lacey, satin curtain, Claire still dressed in pajamas, is standing. He doesn't acknowledge her even though their eyes meet. He quickly speeds out of the driveway, narrowly missing the green mailbox in his path.

He drives through the familiar town and arrives to the department store that he has visited many times. He checks his watch. 8:04. The store has just opened so it is thankfully not busy. He dashes in and quickly finds a pair of dress pants in his size and a button down shirt to match. After he rings out his purchases, he makes the dreadful drive to his office. He attempts to sneak in the back door so only a few people see him. Only the secretary spots him and when he avoids her smile and "hello!" she takes the hint and pretends not to see him.

He unlocks the door and slides in. He shuts the door behind him. He doesn't initially turn on a light but walks around in the darkness. He can hear a few voices outside but the darkness inside is almost calming. He does several laps around the tiny room before walking over to the light switch. He flips it on. He blinks several times to help his eyes adjust to the difference in brightness.

Before anyone has a chance to knock on his door, he quickly changes into his newly acquired clothes. Just as he is rearranging his tie, there is a quiet but noticeable knock on the door. He takes a look at himself in his only available mirror to make sure he looks presentable before opening it. It's his assistant.

"Good morning, sir. You're looking a little rough. Can I get you some coffee?"

Cam is a little taken aback by Veronica's sudden niceness. "Oh, ummm." he purposely hesitates waiting for a rude comment to interrupt him. When one does not follow, he continues. "Sure, that would be nice. Thanks."

The petite red head turns around and disappears. Cam shakes his head in bewilderment. He walks out into the narrow hallway and into the reception area. He grabs the first file and flips through it. Before he has time to get to the last page, the assistant has placed six more files on the counter. Sitting on top of the pile is a steaming mug of coffee.

"Really? We're that busy this early?" Cam says annoyed.

He pokes his head through the reception window. Not surprisingly, the room is already full of waiting patients. He takes a deep breath, balls up his fists tightly then relaxes them. He sighs extra loud, causing a nearby physician to look up and smile.

"Yeah, going to be another long day."

"Yeah," Cam unhappily agrees.

He spends the rest of his scheduled half day quickly going through his many patients. No sooner did the last patient check out of the office, Cam checks out as well. He grabs his jacket and his old clothes and heads out of the back door. He puts everything into his car and is just about to climb in the driver side when he changes his mind. The bright sun invites him to walk instead. He heads to the sidewalk and walks along with the flow of traffic. The warm breeze feels nice even though he is already dressed rather warm. He stops walking and steps to the side to allow a mother with a double wide stroller pass by without trouble. He nods at her and smiles.

The road is very busy on this particular day, with people getting off work. He glances down at his watch. CJ should probably be getting home soon, he thinks. He gets a rush of different emotions. He's sad, but happy; anxious but angry all at the same time. He used to be happy and content with every aspect of his life, including his family and job. Now his son is the only thing that makes him feel that way.

Do I go home to see CJ, he wonders, only to deal with Claire's wrath later? Or should I wait until CJ and Claire go to bed? Cam imagines the look of disappointment on CJ's face and this helps make his decision much easier. He turns around and begins to head back to his car. Then he gets an idea. He turns back around and continues on the busy sidewalk. After several minutes, he arrives at a small, hole-in-the-wall bakery. He doesn't hesitate going inside, knowing the greeting that awaits him.

"Cammy!"

Cam's eyes quickly scan the room until his eyes fall onto a short, stout, and balding man. His dark, thick rimmed glasses sit lazily on the edge of his very pointed noise. As soon as he spots Cameron, he walks out from behind his display case. He brushes what Cam can only speculate is flour on his hands off onto his apron.

"Kevin! How are you? How are the kids?" They shake hands and Cam clearly listens to his friend update him on his family business. He checks his watch and realizes how late it is. "Oh, I really need to be going. Can I get the usual, please?"

The disappointed baker replies, "Sure. Two chocolate cupcakes and two peanut butter cupcakes, coming right up." The enthusiasm is lost from his voice. Cameron paces for the short time it takes the man to bag the fresh, large desserts.

"Thanks, Kev. How much do I owe you?"

"Don't worry about it. You can owe me later. Tell Claire I said 'hello.'"

"Ok, will do." As he says this, he rolls his eyes. He tries to smile and sound genuine but he is aware of this lack of emotion. He grabs the white bag and heads back out onto the sidewalk.

Although the sun is now hiding behind several darkening clouds, it is still bright and warm outside. Each step he takes on the busy sidewalk brings him one step closer toward his withdrawn but loving, gentle, and insightful child. Those same steps, however, take him one step closer to the cold, cheating, lying, and manipulative woman he once trusted.

He can't help but feel sad. His relationship with his family is changing. All of the fond memories he has come flooding back to him, including the many times they ate these very cupcakes out on the back porch and drank chocolate milk. He feels the tears begin to creep into his eyes. He quickly brushes them away before anyone can see them.

Several loud screams from behind him snaps him out of his daze. He turns around just in time to see a car coming straight towards him. He has no time to react as it smashes into his legs. He catapults into the air and after he bounces off the trunk, lands on his stomach on the sidewalk. He lies on the cement. He uses his remaining strength to open his eyes halfway. He tries to look around but blood pools in front of his eyes. He closes them; no longer having the strength to open them again.

JULIA

"What are you guys watching?"

"Just some stupid movie," Julia says. She scoots a little closer to Allen. Without an invitation, her mother walks over and plops down on the now empty cushion.

"Do you guys want something to eat?"

"No, Mom," Julia says, frustrated. Ever since Jossa's boyfriend was arrested a few days ago, Jossa has been crowding Julia more than usual. "When does he get out?" Julia asks, hoping it is sooner rather than later.

"I don't know. You know he hasn't tried to call me yet? If you care about someone, you should at least call them; even if it's from jail."

"Mom, why don't you leave him alone? He's not a nice guy. You don't need someone like that anyway."

"Oh, like Allen is good for you."

As she says this, Allen jumps to his feet. "What does that mean? What's your problem? Run out of alcohol already?"

Jossa jumps to her feet, startling Julia. "I graduated high school, can you say that? I didn't get left by both my parents, did you?"

Julia winces. Allen is very sensitive about his situation with his parents. Knowing the conversation is only going to get worse, Julia leaps to her feet and makes sure to stand between her mother and boyfriend. "Guys, cool it. Allen, let's just go."

"No," Allen says, determined to win the battle. "Keep on talking, you old hag."

Jossa takes a step toward her daughter's boyfriend. "Don't mind if I do."

"Ok, but I mind it." Julia is beginning to feel uneasy. "Both of you, seriously, knock it off." Panic is starting to settle in when she sees no one is willing to back down. "Allen, why don't we go for a walk." She grabs his arm and tries to pull him toward the front door and away from her mother.

"You go take a walk. You're really pissing me off anyway," Allen jerks his arm out of her grip.

Julia gives up and leaves the apartment. They've argued in the past and Julia couldn't break them up then either. She walks down the street to her friend's house. She walks up the few steps to the front porch. She lifts her hand to knock on the front door but it opens before she gets the opportunity.

"Hey, girl, long time no see." A teenager, only slightly younger than Julia, greets her.

"Oh, Allen and Jossa are at it again. I hate when they fight. I'm so afraid something is going to happen to one of them."

"Nothing is going to happen."

"Nik, you don't know that for sure, though. You didn't see the look on either one of their faces. It was horrible."

Nikki takes a step back and allows Julia to enter her house. Julia quickly accepts and walks in. Although it is light outside, the inside is dark. The living room is rather large. The dark green carpet is highly stained with brown spots and the minimal furniture is not in any better condition.

"Want a soda or anything?" Nikki asks as she shuts the front door.

"Ummm, sure. I don't care what it is. What do you think I should do about my mom and Allen, though?"

"Jul, listen to me. There's nothing you can really do. Unless you kick Allen or your mother out, they are always going to be around each other. They need to learn to get along or just leave. Stop worrying about it."

Julia sits down on the couch. "Dude, this couch stinks." She stands back up and looks down. Nothing appears to be spilled but the scent is awful.

"Yeah, my neighbor came over and brought her cat. He peed all over the couch."

Julia looks appalled at her friend. "Did you clean it up?"

"Yeah, of course. Well, sort of. I didn't really have anything to use but paper towels."

"Oh, Nikki. That's so gross. Why didn't you call me? I would have brought you something. This is so gross."

"Oh well, nothing I can do now. Want to watch a movie? I was planning on watching this cute, romantic one."

"Sure, but I think I'm going to sit on the floor."

"Hey, I actually just got a folding chair. It's in the kitchen. Go sit on that, the floor is probably pretty gross, too."

Julia thankfully walks into the kitchen. The tiny kitchen is extremely cluttered. Next to the sink is a wooden chair. She takes one step toward it but stops. Her left foot gets wet when she steps into a large puddle. She jumps back and groans at the same time. She lifts her foot. Although it appears to just be water, Julia is still disgusted. She gingerly places her wet foot back onto the floor. She disgustedly grabs the chair, at least thankful she doesn't have to sit on the floor. She walks back into the living room and sits down next to her friend.

"Nik, your house is absolutely disgusting."

"Clean it."

Irritated, Julia continues to sit quietly. After a half an hour, Julia's phone vibrates in her pocket. Expecting it to be either Allen or her mother, she withdraws her phone. The caller ID says *Work*. "Oh, thank God," she says aloud. She gets to her feet and excuses herself to the kitchen. After a few minutes, she reenters the living room.

"Looks like I'm going to have to leave. Just got called into work."

"Sure you did, put the chair back before you leave."

Although Nikki couldn't see her, Julia shakes her head. She walks over to her spot and picks up the chair. It squeaks loudly as she folds it up. She was halfway to the kitchen when she remembers the disgusting floor. The idea of standing in that puddle twice in one day is too much. She sits the chair against the wall in the hallway. She turns around and leaves the house without saying another word to Nikki.

The sunny weather is still nice and welcoming. She makes a quick dash back to her apartment to get her work clothes. She opens the door to the apartment, momentarily forgetting about the riff between her mother and boyfriend. Although everything is quiet now, the aftermath of the argument is evident. The few pictures that were on the wall now lay broken and in pieces on the floor. Glass is shattered by her bedroom door and Julia has to dance around it. Two of the three cushions on the couch are strewn across the room, the other one is messily laying next to the couch. The coffee table is flipped over on its side; Allen's favorite thing to do when he gets upset. There are a few drops of blood on the carpet as well. This makes Julia nervous. Whose blood is it? She doesn't know what she's hoping for; her mother or boyfriend.

"Hello?" she pauses. "Mom? Are you here? Mom? Allen?"

There's nothing but silence. Julia jogs the short distance to Jossa's bedroom. She pushes open the door, thankful to find the room empty. She stands in the doorway, pondering where they went. Trying not to look into it anymore, she runs to her room and changes her clothes. She quickly runs a brush through her hair and leaves the tiny apartment, making sure to lock the door behind her.

She walks down the sidewalk. Although it is the middle of the day, no one is outside enjoying the sunshine. She arrives at the small deli but cannot bring herself to go in. Her mind is spinning with thoughts and problems. She doesn't realize she's pacing until her manager steps outside.

"Are you alright?" Although he's usually a happy, go-lucky man, today his voice is full of concern.

Julia stops her mindless pacing and stares at the thirty-something man. His blue polo shirt is tucked perfectly into his black work pants. She notices his smile but doesn't return it. For a moment, she considers being honest.

"Yeah, I'm fine," she decidedly lies. She tries to sound convincing but when she clearly fails, she adds, "just the usual."

"Ok, well, if you're feeling better, we really need to head inside."

He smiles at her slightly but then turns around and heads into the deli. Julia waits for the door to shut entirely before muttering to herself, "Maybe today was a mistake." She forces herself to take a deep breath and throws her hands up on top of her head. After allowing herself to enjoy a wave of cool breeze, she walks into the deli. Although there are not many customers eating, there is at least double that number waiting in line. She sighs and jumps behind the counter next to the manager. They do not speak to one another for the next fifteen minutes as they push the line of customers through. After the last customer is handed their food, Jordan breaks the silence.

"Thanks for coming in to help. I definitely wouldn't have made it through without you. Madison called off again. Matt is still planning on coming in soon, though."

"That's fine. I'm going to run to the bathroom."

She excuses herself before Jordan can say no. She scurries to the bathroom and quickly shuts the door. She throws herself onto the toilet. With her elbows on her knees and rests her head on her hands. I shouldn't be here, she thinks. I can't do this. She tries to put herself back together before she exits the restroom. She glances back to the counter and sees Jordan is once again overwhelmed by hungry customers. She sighs and slowly walks over. In a daze, she quietly fixes up several sandwiches. Mustering up the courage to tell the manager she needs to leave, she turns to face him. She takes a deep breath and opens her mouth to speak.

A loud screech followed by a crash interrupts her. It shocks everyone in the deli and it becomes instantly quiet. No one can move at first but when Jordan moves to the front door, everyone follows suit. They all stare anxiously outside and see a small car swerving back and forth on the busy road. Still at a high rate of speed, the car heads towards the tiny deli. Taking charge of the situation, Jordan pushes everyone away from the window. They all brace themselves for the impact.

Crash.

The loud collision causes the tiny deli to tremble but there is no shattering glass and definitely no car in the entrance. Julia doesn't move from her spot next to the counter. She watches as Jordan takes several leery steps toward the door. Julia is shaking as she stands next to several patrons. She cannot bring herself to move because she knows her legs will give out. As she watches Jordan take another step toward the front door, it flies open. A tall, dirty and slightly bloody man stumbles in. Julia backs up so her back presses gently against the counter. She's stunned. She stares at him, unsure if she should make sure he's alright. When the man has been inside for just a few seconds, he raises his hand over his head. She sees the gun. Her heart pounds in her chest.

"Everyone needs to move against this wall," he says.

She looks in the direction of where he's pointing. She makes a move to head in that direction but when no one else moves, she freezes. When the man sees that no one is listening, he shouts, "EVERYONE MOVE!"

Julia doesn't need to be told again. She scurries across the deli to the far wall and sits down on the hard floor. She pulls her knees to her chest and tries to keep herself from throwing up. She looks around the room, searching for Jordan. She finds him at the other end of the line of people. He catches her eye and tries to signal reassurance with his gaze. It doesn't help this time. She focuses on trying not to puke.

"Please let us go," she finally musters.

"I don't want to hear anyone right now."

"But sir…"

"But sir," the gunman mimics in a high pitched voice. He waves his gun in the air. Julia throws her arms over her head and squeezes her eyes shut.

"Sorry," she mumbles, unsure if it is going to help the situation. She pauses before moving her arms away from her head. She looks at the other people surrounding her. They are all quiet. Not only does the silence spread amongst the group but their heads are down, staring at the floor. She follows suit. After a minute, Julia looks up. The man sits back down but he is mumbling to himself. She can't help but stare at him. His hands are shaking. Blood is dripping from his busted nose.

The phone inside the deli begins to ring. Julia jumps at the sudden loud noise. When the phone rings for the third time, Carl, a regular at the deli says, "Well, you should probably answer the phone."

The strange man runs over to Carl and smacks him in the face with the butt of the gun. Julia gasps. She scoots as far away from him as she possibly can. Her eyes fill with tears and her heart feels as though it may pound out of her chest at any moment.

"Anyone else feel like I should answer the phone?"

Julia quickly shakes her head no. This causes several tears to fall down her already damp cheek.

"I didn't think so," the man adds.

The gunman dashes back behind the deli counter, Julia scoots next to Jordan. She links her arm into his and rests her head onto his broad shoulder. She begins shaking uncontrollably. She starts breathing heavier. She tries to force herself to calm down but it's not working. When the phone rings for the second time, Julia gets a large knot in her stomach.

"Oh my Lord!"

The man screams out, terrifying Julia even more. She watches him grab the phone and rip it out of the wall. It immediately stops ringing. He stands up and throws it with all his might at the large, glass entrance. The glass shatters instantly. There is a loud ruckus outside that resonates in.

Julia watches the glass fall to the ground as if in slow motion. It bounces back into the air for a moment before it lands back to the ground, breaking into even smaller pieces. She looks over at the man and his back is against the opposite wall. He seems distracted. Taking that as a sign, Julia leaps to her feet and runs as fast as she can to the broken door. She anticipates gun fire but when it doesn't happen, she runs faster. She's careful not to look behind her. She gets to the door and can't help but trip over the glass. She can see police cars lining the streets and paramedics are located down the street. A large, heavy set police officer springs toward her. She gets a little nervous but elated at the same time. She quickly places her hands on her head as he reaches her. He grabs her hands and leads her down the sidewalk, away from the deli.

"Thank you," she mumbles.

"Hey, you!"

Julia snaps back to reality and looks around the room. She's still sitting in the deli. Her heart sinks down to her stomach. "Hey, you!" he repeats. When Julia looks in his direction, he points his gun her way. "What's your name?"

"Me?" Julia asks with terror in her voice. She looks around to the other people, hoping he is referring to someone else.

"Yes. I asked you a question."

"O-o-hh, ummm, it's Julia, sir."

"Alright, Julia. Is there another way out of here?"

She considers for a second whether or not to answer. Glancing at the gun in the man's hand, she chooses to answer. "There is a back door the employees use. You can try that."

"Good. Show me."

Julia stands up slowly. Her knees are shaking and they are barely able to hold her. As soon as she gets to her feet, the man reaches out and grabs her arm. She thinks about pulling away but is scared of the retaliation. She has no time to gather her thoughts. When they began walking to the back of the deli, the man holds Julia directly in front of himself like a human shield. He forces her into the tiny hallway. They both take a few steps into the dark hallway. He lets go of her arm and Julia watches as he throws open the back door. Although the brightness blinds her, she can tell coming back here is a mistake. She takes a step back and awaits the gunfire. The hallway darkens again but there are no gun shots.

"The cops are already out there, aren't they?"

Julia nods her head.

"Get back in there with the rest of the group."

Julia doesn't wait for any more direction. She turns around and heads back into the main room of the deli. Her stomach hops into her throat. The deli is empty. The last of the patrons are running out of the front door. She watches as Jordan hops over large pieces of glass that cover the ground. She tries to look behind the counter to see if the rest of the people are hiding back there. Although she can't see from where she is standing, she knows there is no one back there. They all left her with him. She forces herself to look at the man. He, too, saw the group leave the deli through the broken door.

"No! No! No!" she hears him mutter.

The sound of a megaphone interrupts her panicked thoughts.

"My name is Officer Hank Evans. You can just call me Hank. I want to know if you're willing to talk to us for a minute. We just want to help you. I'm going to call you again and I'd really like it if you'd answer."

Julia hears him snicker to himself.

"Well, that's going to be pretty difficult since we have no phone," he says quietly but loud enough for Julia to hear. After giving Julia's arm a quick yank behind the meat counter, he continues. "Looks like it's just going to be you and me now. Lucky you."

Julia can't speak. Even if she could, she'd probably just throw up. Her mind races with many thoughts and questions. Is he going to let her go? Is he going to kill her? Does he *plan* on killing her? Should she try to convince him to let her go, too? Why didn't her friend wait for her? He just abandoned her to deal with the crazy man by herself.

"This is Officer Evans again. We know there are still more people inside. Why don't you let them go and we can talk."

Julia's head perks up. Maybe this officer can convince him to let her go, she thinks hopefully. She watches him stand up. She wonders if she should follow suit. She doesn't have to wonder for long.

"Stand up."

She slowly gets up and hugs herself. She begins to shiver from nerves. She cannot bring herself to look at him.

"Start walking," he says to her.

She pauses. "I-I-I don't know where you want me to go."

"Well, you want to leave, don't you?"

Her heart starts beating faster. She refuses to let herself get too excited. There must be a catch to this. She forces herself to make the eye contact she is dreading. "Well, yes."

"Ok, the door is that way." With the gun still tightly in his hand, he points to the shattered door. She forces her legs to move even though they feel like jelly. She feels as though her heart is going to pound out of her chest. Her hands begin to shake violently. She walks past him, trying hard to avoid touching him. When she feels his arm brush against hers, she shivers again. She gingerly walks to the front door, expecting him to change his mind. She gets to the entrance way and looks out at the crowd of people that have gathered. Police cars with the lights flashing, stare at her. Julia can see people standing on the sidewalk to the left of the deli. They are all standing behind a police line. She draws in a quick breath when she sees what she perceives as hundreds of guns pointing in her direction. She wants to scream out, 'Please don't shoot me!' but she instead stays quiet.

"Alright, Mark, you're doing the right thing."

When nothing more is said or done, Julia decides to make the first move. She takes another step toward freedom. When no gunshots ring out, she continues to take another step, but can't. Mark is holding onto the back of her shirt preventing her from making an escape. Although she didn't realize it is possible, her heart beats faster.

"I want a deal," Julia hears Mark yell to the only officer standing without a shield.

Officer Evans does not hesitate with his response. "Sir," he says just as loud as Mark. "Let the girl go and we will make any deal we can."

Julia can feel the grasp on her shirt loosen. She takes a few slow steps forward. She's leery but desperate to get away from Mark. The more steps she takes, the more confident she becomes. After her fifth step, two loud *pops* ring out and a hot pain shoots through her body. She gets to take one more step towards her freedom before she is overcome with darkness and falls to the sidewalk.

MARK

He walks up to the counter. He tries to appear nonchalant as he hands over the prescription. He smiles at the young but very beautiful woman. She glances down at the crinkled paper then looks back at him.

"I don't know if we have this. Give me a minute." She gives him a half smile and walks back around the counter. Unsure of what to do with himself, Mark jams his hands into the front pockets of his dirty jeans. Mark watches as she hands the fake prescription over to the man with the white coat. The slightly older man looks it over and looks up at Mark.

"We have this so we'll fix it up for you. It's going to be about half an hour. Just listen for your name over the loud speaker."

"Oh, ok. Thanks, guys."

Trying not to push his luck, Mark turns around and leaves the small, cluttered pharmacy. He begins looking around the even smaller store. A woman and her two kids seem to be the only other customers shopping. They should be out of the store in half an hour, he thinks to himself. The only thing Mark worries about is occupying himself for the half an hour while not drawing much attention. These drug store trips were always easier when he had someone with him. He felt much more confident.

The tiny store is somewhat of a wreck. The floor is dirty and covered in crumbs of food, puddles of water or soda, and swirls of mud. The shelves are messily arranged with boxes of crackers neighboring both toilet bowel cleaner with dish towels. The temperature of the store is much higher than the temperature outside. He realizes this as he begins to sweat. He walks around to the other side of the store. He pretends to look interested in the price of toothbrushes.

"Can I help you?"

Mark whips around, startling both himself and the young man standing behind him.

"Nope, I'm just waiting for my prescription."

"Ok," the man says with fake enthusiasm. The man leans onto the adjacent shelf. "Just let me know if you need something." His pearly white teeth glisten as brightly as the gold on his employee name tag. It reads *Morgan.*

"Alrightly, Morgan, will do." He places extra emphasis onto the employee's name. Mark considers saying 'thank you' but decides against it. When Morgan gets out of eye sight, Mark drops the toothbrush onto the ground. It skips twice then comes to rest near his right foot. He kicks it, sending it sliding across the crud-infested floor. The longer he waits, the more anxious he becomes. He glances down at his watch; only about half the time has elapsed since he dropped off the prescription. Frustrated, he wanders down the candy aisle. He locates several of his favorite sweets and quickly shoves them into his jacket pocket.

As if someone overhead is watching his actions, a voice shouts out over the speaker, "Miller to the pharmacy."

Hearing the fake name aloud, Mark instantly turns around and heads straight back to the pharmacy. When he gets there, the pharmacist is standing at the counter, seemingly waiting for him. Mark plasters on a smile but he's the only one. He gets to the counter and rests his hands on the countertop.

"Mr. Miller, I cannot fill this prescription. I called the doctor to verify it and they haven't seen anybody in their office with that name."

Mark sighs both deeply and loudly. "So what are we going to do about this? I really need these meds."

"Sir, you really need to leave."

"I need that medication."

Mark looks up at the young technician. She looks away and refuses to make eye contact. Mark's adrenaline begins to kick in. He leans over the counter a little closer to the pharmacist. The pharmacist doesn't move. The two men stare at one another for a few seconds. Finally, Mark outstretches his hand for the prescription. When the pharmacist continues to stand as still as a statue, Mark grabs the pharmacist's large wrist. Mark can feel him tighten up slightly and pull back. Mark opens the front of his jacket and flashes the small gun in his waist band.

"This was supposed to be easy," Mark says, lowering his voice. "I want those pills. You have two minutes before I make you regret coming into work today." Mark releases the man's arm.

The now less confident pharmacist stumbles backward. Mark watches as he walks quickly behind the counter. He ducks around the corner, out of sight.

"Absolutely not," Mark shouts. "I can't see you. Get back out here."

The pharmacist pops back out. "I have to unlock the drawer, so I have to go back here."

Mark thinks for a second. "Make it quick." He looks at the young woman again. Her stare jumps from him, to the counter, to the pharmacist, and back to him. Mark can hear the sound of a metal cabinet opening. As soon as the door opens, the pharmacist reappears. He hesitates, then slowly asks, "What do you want?"

"Don't be stupid. Give me everything."

The pharmacist disappears again and Mark can hear lots of bottles being thrown into a plastic bag. The man reappears in front of Mark. He looks inside the bag, takes a deep breath, then hands the bag over to Mark.

Mark snatches the bag out of his hand. Their eyes meet. In a split second, Mark aims the gun and quickly pulls the trigger. A shrill scream follows the crash. He turns around and his stomach jumps into his throat. Standing closer than he anticipated is the woman with the two, small children. He stops in his tracks. The woman instantly grabs her children and pushes them behind her. The two adults lock eyes. Neither one blinks. Neither one says a word. The woman takes a step back. Her children do the same. The child on the left begins to cry. This breaks the eye contact between Mark and the woman. She glances down at her child then looks up at Mark.

"Please…"

With both adrenaline and panic settling in, Mark raises the gun. Before he can stop himself, he pulls the trigger several times. He stands there watching the woman crumple to the ground. Before the woman hits the filthy ground, Mark sees a small body hit first. The second child begins screaming. Mark dashes out of the store and runs to the car. He almost drops his bag of stolen medication as he opens the car door. He jumps in, throwing the bag and gun onto the passenger seat. He turns on his mother's big boat of a car. The engine struggles to keep turning. He places it in reverse and backs out of the parking lot. He doesn't pay attention and backs into another parked car. He pauses for a second then throws the car into drive. The tires squeal as he peels out of the parking lot and onto the main road.

He takes a deep breath and tries to calm his racing heart. He glances down at the bag on the seat next to him. He leans over and opens the bag. He smiles when he sees the contents.

"Perfect," he says a loud.

Things didn't go as planned but getting the bag is well worth it. Wait until his friends hear that he had a successful trip by himself. The image of the tiny body falling to the floor flashes into his mind. Almost successful, he thinks. He reaches into the bag and withdraws a bottle. Taking his eyes off the road, he opens the bottle and pops a small handful of tablets into his house. Readjusting his car on the road, he reaches into the center console and pulls out a small half-empty bottle of vodka. He washes down the pills with several gulps. A calmness begins to settle over him.

He turns his attention back to the road. There are hardly any other cars driving on the street. He leans back in his seat and gets comfortable. He lets his mind wander to what he's going to do with his new prized bag. He'll have to decide which ones to keep for himself and which ones he's going to sell. He glances down at his speedometer. 75 mph. He considers slowing down as not to draw attention to himself but changes his mind. Feeling invincible, he presses down on the gas pedal and the car speeds through the residential neighborhood. He takes his eyes off the road for a few seconds to adjust the radio. After recognizing a song, he cranks up the volume. Although the old car cannot handle the loud, over powering bass, he turns the knob on the volume all the way up. The car shakes and rattles as cars and buildings whiz by him. As he nears the busier part of town, he pushes the gas pedal even harder. He crosses the double yellow line several times in an attempt to avoid slowing down. He glances in his rearview mirror. A set of bright red and blue lights begin to flash in his eyes.

"Damn it!" he shouts. His voice is drowned out by the sounds of the radio. Quickly making the decision to not pull over, he takes his eyes off the mirror. He continues to weave in and out of the cars. As he nears the intersection, the traffic light overhead goes from green, to yellow, then abruptly to red. He speeds up. The loud music not only fuels his adrenaline but it hides the sound of the multiple car horns that blare in his direction. He continues swerving through traffic.

He begins to lose control of the high-speed vehicle. He attempts to slow down but it's too late. He looks behind him and sees several more police cars speeding along with him. He begins sliding back and forth, narrowly missing other cars. Up ahead, traffic has come to a halt. He slams on the brakes. His tires squeal as he attempts to slow down. Before he has time to react, the car uncontrollably jerks to the left. There are several cars coming toward him. He grips the wheel tighter while pressing the brakes harder. A large car is in his path and he tries desperately to miss it. Panicking, he over compensates and spins the wheel too sharply to the left. He manages to avoid a head on collision and side swipes the driver side instead. The other car reacts to the collision by turning a sharp 45 degree angle. It strikes a telephone pole. Mark is oblivious to the loud '*bang*' resonating from the crash. His focus is still trying to take control of his car. He fails. The car shoots across the next lane of traffic and onto the adjoining sidewalk. With his foot still on the brake, the smell of burning tires smack him in the face. The few people walking on the sidewalk scamper away from the car; everyone except a middle-aged man. His body smashes into the hood of the car and flies over the roof. The damaged car finally comes to a stop when it plows into a utility pole.

He allows himself several seconds to gather his thoughts. His head is pounding from the impact of the air bag. He puts his hand to his nose. When he pulls his hand away, he sees his hand is covered in blood. He turns to the right and the gun had fallen to the floor of the front seat. He reaches down and plucks it up. Police cars are beginning to arrive so he jumps out of the crashed vehicle, leaving the pharmacy bag on the floor. He wobbles on his shaking legs. Unsure of what to do, he dashes into the nearest building.

He makes sure the door closes behind him. Panting hard, he looks around. There are not many people inside. No one says a word. They all remain silent and stare at the strange man. Realizing he needs to get far away from the glass doors, he holds his hand up high, raising the gun over his head.

"Everyone needs to move against this wall," he says quickly, pointing to the wall next to the table and chairs. At first, no one moves. "EVERYONE! MOVE!"

No more prodding is needed as everyone quickly moves to the far wall. Once they are all situated, Mark darts behind the counter. From this viewpoint, he can keep his eye on his new hostages and on the door to the deli. He can see police cars surrounding the building and their lights glare off the clean window. He kneels down, wiping the sweat off his brow. Seven sets of eyes are seemingly boring a hole into him.

"Please let us go," a quiet, timid girl calls out to him.

"I don't want to hear anyone right now."

"But sir," the persistent girl interrupts.

Mark jumps to his feet, waving his gun in the air. Realizing what he's doing, he hits the ground faster than when he jumped up. He peeks his head around the counter but he doesn't see any cops in the doorway.

"What to do, what to do," he mumbles to himself. Using his sleeve, he wipes the blood from his nose.

The phone rings.

It makes everyone in the room jump. After the 3rd thing, an older, heavy set man says, "Well, you should probably answer the phone."

Mark lunges at the man, roughly socking him in the face with his gun. A small group of people gasp. The stranger slumps down against the wall, blood trickling down his face. A mother and daughter scoot backwards away from both the injured man and Mark.

"Anyone else feel like I should answer the phone?" Mark sees the rest of the group shake their head. "I didn't think so."

He quickly walks back to his spot behind the counter. The phone stops ringing after the eleventh ring. Before Mark can get comfortable with the silence, it rings again.

"Oh my Lord!"

He reaches over and rips the phone out of the wall. The ringing is cut abruptly short. He stands up and with all his strength, throws it at the glass door. He ducks back behind the counter as a loud crash echoes inside. He runs his left hand through his hair, trying to think of a way out.

"Hey, you!" he points his gun at the young deli worker. "What's your name?"

"Me?" the girl points to herself but still looks around to the other people.

"Yes. I asked you a question."

"O-o-ohh, ummm, it's Julia, sir."

"Alrighty, Julia. Is there another way out of here?"

"There is a back door the employees use." Mark can see her eyes are on the gun only.

"Good. Show me."

Julia stands up slowly. As soon as she gets to her feet, Mark reaches out and grabs her arm. She's shaking slightly. He makes sure to put her between himself and the cops outside. He leads her through the back door and they disappear into a small hallway. The only thing in the tiny hallway is another door in front of him. He releases Julia's arm and without thinking, flings open the back door. Sunlight pours in and the sudden burst of light shocks him. Before his eyes have time to fully adjust, he gets the feeling he's not alone. He takes a step back and hurriedly shuts the door. Now that he's more aware of his surroundings, he can hear the noise of many people talking outside.

"The cops are already out there, aren't they?" He watches Julia nod her head. "Get back in there with the rest of the group."

They turn around and head back through the door to the deli. Julia pushes open the door. Mark stops in surprise. No one is sitting on the floor where he left them. He looks at the door and sees the last of the customers running out of the door, jumping over the large shards of glass.

"No, no, no, no!" Mark screams. His mind is racing and his palms are getting sweaty as the seconds tick by.

A loud, deep voice being magnified by a megaphone, echoes. "Hi. My name is Officer Hank Evans. I want to know if you're willing to talk to us for a minute. We just want to help you. I'm going to call you again but I'd really like it if you'd answer the phone this time."

Knowing Officer Evans cannot hear him, he says, "Well, dumbass, that's going to be a little hard since we have no phone." He grabs Julia's arm again and yanks her down behind the counter. "Looks like it's just going to be you and me now. Lucky you," he adds.

His comment is met with more silence.

Mark sits against the wall, trying to think of this next move.

"Hello! This is Officer Evans again. We know there are still more people inside. Why don't you let them go and we can talk?"

Out of the corner of his eye, he can see Julia looking at him. He runs through different scenarios in his head. None, however, include him walking out of here alive. He can feel his anxiety climbing. With no other option, he slowly gets to his feet. He looks down at his hostage. She is leaning against the wall with her knees drawn up to her chest.

He pushes his feelings of sympathy and regret back down and coldly says, "Stand up."

He can see the hesitation but she stands up. She wraps her arms around herself and refuses to make eye contact.

"Start walking," Mark says.

"I-I-I don't know where you want me to go."

Mark is surprised by her reluctance.

"Well, you want to leave, don't you?"

She finally makes eye contact. "Well, yes."

"Ok, the door is that way." With the gun in his hand, he points to the broken front door. She walks around him. Mark takes a step back to give her more space. Mark gingerly walks to the front door, making sure to stay directly behind her. Mark can see many police cars and people outside. When Mark sees more guns than faces, he tenses up. He can feel Julia react the same way. The noise outside seems to completely stop. Time stands still once everyone realizes the couple is arriving at the door.

A tall, young looking man with sandy, brown hair and a large megaphone emerges from one of the vehicles. "Alright, Mark, you're doing the right thing."

Mark grips her shirt tighter to keep her in place. When she takes a step forward, Mark pulls her back. He shouts over her head to the crowd of officers. "I want a deal."

Officer Evans responds quickly. "Sir, let the girl go and we will make any deal we can."

Hesitantly, Mark lets go of the blue, cotton, shirt. With that, Julia takes a few steps away from Mark and a few steps closer to freedom. As Julia walks away, Mark has a clearer view of what's in front of him. Eight police cars and one police SUV with their lights glowing red and blue, shine back at him. Men are standing behind the car and kneeling behind opened doors. All are brandishing guns in his direction. Although the warm sun is shining, cold chills run up and down his body. This causes him to shiver. He considers reaching out and plucking Julia off the sidewalk and back into the deli. Instead, he uncovers his gun and quickly pulls the trigger several times. He doesn't get a chance to regain his composure. The response to his shots are answered by an array of gunfire. He doesn't have the opportunity to fall to the ground before his world goes dark.

THE END

MARK

Mark slowly opens his eyes. He looks around, still feeling significantly dazed. He looks to the left and sees a beat up, plush orange and brown recliner sitting in a recognizable spot. Just to confirm what he thinks, he looks in the opposite direction. Sitting to the right is a large over-sized TV placed oddly in the TV stand. It is clearly not meant to hold such weight due to its progressive lean to one side. After a moment, all the pieces fall into place. He's lying on the floor in his own living room.

"How strange," he says quietly to himself.

"What's strange?" a voice calls out.

Mark jumps to his feet. The room spins, causing him to stop and regain his balance. When he doesn't initially see anyone, he feels himself begin to panic. He tries to force himself to act tough.

"Who is in my house?"

Extremely proud of his masculinity, he flexes his muscles. He still chooses to walk slowly and timidly to the next room.

"It's just me."

The voice is getting closer with every step Mark takes. It seems to be coming from the dining room. Mark looks around the living room, searching for anything he can use as a weapon. He sees a short, skinny, blue lamp. Better than nothing, he thinks. He bends down and unplugs it from the adjoining wall. He attempts to lift it from the side table but he cannot. At first, he thinks it is a little heavier than he originally planned but after a few hard yanks, it still doesn't move. It's frozen on the table as though it has been glued down. Confused, he abandons the lamp. It's useless anyway. He sees nothing else he can use. Taking a deep breath, he balls up his fists and puffs out his chest. He walks into the dining room. Although the room is already filled with natural, outdoor light, Mark turns on the overhead light. Unsure of what he's going to see, he braces himself for anything.

Sitting at the round table is a tall, well-built, middle-aged man. His soft blonde hair is cut short and his bright, sparkling blue eyes greet the very confused Mark. The only other item on the table is a cream colored coffee mug. Even from his far distance, Mark can see steam billowing from the top. The man is wearing a tattered pair of jeans and a well ironed black t-shirt. He has a short goatee and thick rimmed glasses.

"What are you doing in my house?"

"Just hanging out. How're you feeling?"

Without thinking, Mark responds, "Fine. I feel fine. Get out." When the mysterious man says nothing and refuses to move a muscle, Mark snaps. He lunges forward and grabs the collar of the stranger's shirt. In the process, the coffee spills on himself, the table, and the intruder.

Neither person seems phased by the spill. Mark forcefully stands the man up. He hesitates for only a moment then places both hands on the man's chest. Mark shoves him with such force, the man topples backward. He falls to the ground. Mark wastes no time in running over to the fallen stranger. Mark picks him back up. He grips the man's shirt tightly in one hand while swiftly raising his other hand. Mark swings his fist hard. He somehow finds the extra strength to stop himself within inches of the man's face. The man does not flinch. He continues to stand still, staring intently at Mark. There's a small smile on his face and even his eyes are smiling. The panic he originally felt has completely disappeared. His anger is rising. As the seconds slowly tick by, he gets madder. He can feel his face getting hot and he fights the urge to wipe the sweat that is now forming on his brow.

"Would you like to sit down yet?" The man speaks calmly. Mark does not feel reassured. He chooses to grip the black shirt. "Relax. Lets talk. I got you some coffee."

Mark looks confusingly down at the table. Sure enough, another steaming mug of coffee is sitting on the table. "How did you..." he lets his voice trail off. "No, thank you."

"If you don't feel like talking then let me show you something. I think you might find it interesting."

"I doubt that," Mark rudely responds. Although he has no idea what is in store, he refuses to agree to anything this man has to offer.

The man reaches out and places his hand onto Mark's hand. Before he realizes what he's doing, Mark releases his shirt. Once Mark releases his cotton hostage, his hands fall down to his side. The cloud of anger is lifting and Mark begins to think logically for the first time since he opened his eyes. Seems like an eternity now. He allows himself to be led by the hand into the living room. Unsure if he should continue walking, he decides to stop. The man, still holding his hand, turns around to face Mark.

"Keep walking, please," he says quietly, calmly, and deliberately to Mark. Mark is beginning to feel anxious again but he reluctantly continues walking through the living room. They arrive at the front door and they both pause. The stranger turns to face Mark for a second time.

"What?" Mark snaps. He is becoming more frustrated. The man doesn't answer Mark's question. He just smiles. "You are just asking me to punch you. What do you want me to do?"

"Open the door, Mark."

Mark groans loudly. He shoves the man, temporarily knocking him off balance. He opens the door. He takes a deep breath and takes a step back. The scene in front of him is nothing he expected. He anticipated seeing the front of his yard. Maybe a car or two driving past. Instead, he is standing inside another building. How is this possible? He was JUST in his living room. He is now standing in the very center of a store. He can see both ends of the tiny place. After a moment, he gets a huge knot in his stomach.

"Oh, God. I know where we are," he says aloud.

The man continues to smile; even broader now. "Come this way."

Mark wants to say no but cannot muster up the word. He allows himself to, once again, be led to the back of the store. As they draw closer, Mark can hear a loud, male voice shouting. Mark slows his pace, in shock of what he is hearing. The voice he hears belongs to none other than himself. When the couple arrive to the back, Mark sees exactly what he's both expecting and dreading. He finds himself staring at a small pharmacy. In front of him is a man standing behind a small counter wearing a white lab coat. Standing on the other side of the counter, with his back to Mark, is a very familiar man. Mark doesn't need the man to turn around to know who it is. It's himself.

The real Mark turns to look at the stranger with him. Unsure of what exactly to say, he manages to spat out, "Wha-what is going on? How did you do this?"

"Mark..."

"I don't know who you are," Mark interrupts. "How do you know my name? I don't know you."

"Mark, you do know me. I know many things you may not. I see many things you may not. I'm going to let you see everything from my perspective."

"I don't care to see..."

"Ssshhh, just watch." This time, the man is the one to interrupt Mark.

As soon as the last word is spoken, everyone in the room hears the loud *bang* of a gunshot. Instinctively, Mark ducks his head. After a few seconds, he remembers what happens next. He immediately stands upright and spins to the right.

He spots the young woman and the two small children. Knowing what is going to ensue, he takes a couple steps toward the family, not sure if he can stop himself from pulling the trigger. A hand reaches out and prevents him from moving forward. Mark jerks his arm from the man's grasp.

"We can't just stand here. He's going to shoot them!" Mark can feel his face redden as severe panic and desperation begins to settle in.

"You mean 'you,' right?"

"Huh?" Mark asks, only half listening.

"You mean 'you' are going to shoot them." The gravity of that statement hits Mark hard. He IS going to shoot them. "There is nothing to stop, it has already happened."

Mark cannot peel his eyes off the two little girls. The terror in their eyes as they cower behind their mother stirs up feelings inside him he hasn't felt in a long time. He feels sick to his stomach as he waits for his past self to raise the gun again. Mark squeezes his eyes shut.

Suddenly, all is quiet. He slowly opens his eyes. He looks around, confused. It was as though everything was frozen. In front of him, he sees the back of his own shirt. He can see the terrified look on the face of the woman as she tries to shield her children.

"Elizabeth."

Mark doesn't say anything. He tears his gaze away from the scene in front of him. He stares at the man.

"That young woman's name is Elizabeth. She is married but not happily. Her husband cares more about the money he makes then the woman he once loved. He's made his point over and over again by beating her in front of their children. The kids you see in front of you are her twin girls. They love to run around and jump in mud puddles. They love to paint and laugh. They are best friends. Although Elizabeth struggles with her relationship with her husband, she unconditionally loves her kids and would sacrifice every-thing for them."

"Listen..."

"Now is not the time to talk," the man interrupts. "Just watch."

The first shot rings out. Mark puts his hands on top of his head. He clenches his teeth and squeezes his eyes as tightly closed as possible.

"Why did I get high? I didn't really need those pills," he mumbles this a few times to himself. Even with his eyes closed, he can see the look on the faces of the little girls. The desperate pleading of the mother as she tries to cover her children, play in his head. Her voice trembles with fear. He opens his eyes and sees the small pile of bodies in front of him. One body begins gasping for air. Mark vomits on the floor. "I gotta get out of here," he says more to himself than to the man.

Without another word, he takes off running for the front door. Although the door is not heavy, he pushes it with all his strength. It flies open, banging against the adjoining wall. The new sight in front of him is not of the parking lot of the tiny store or even of his old neighborhood. In fact, nothing is the same. In front of him is a four lane road. Across the street is not the quiet park he's used to seeing. Instead, businesses line the somewhat busy road. One of Mark's favorite pizza shops stare at him along with a large bank and a thrift shop. He puts one of his hands on his hip and the other one on his forehead.

"Where am I?" he asks quietly, even though he recognizes the sight in front of him. It's part of a nearby town. Even more confused, he turns to the man next to him. "How did we get here? I thought we were at the store. How did we get across town?"

The man doesn't say a word but very calmly smiles. He places one of his hands on Mark's shoulder and looks down the street. Mark starts breathing heavily. He gives a panicked look at the man. He knows what is coming next. Several car horns and loud music alerts Mark to the direction of a small car speeding through traffic. Mark watches as this car weaves from lane to lane. Once the car is directly in front of him, he hears the loud squealing of tires. Mark wants to look away but he can't tear his eyes away. He watches what he knows is the vehicle he's driving, speed along for another moment. It sharply swerves far to the left.

"Slow down!" Mark can't help but yell at the car. He watches his car narrowly miss hitting another car. The stranger's car jerks swiftly in the opposite direction. "Oh, God!" Mark shouts.

Suddenly, a strange silence fills the air. Mark is surprised. Every car in front of him has seemingly stopped in their tracks. He looks around. "How do you do that?" Mark says in amazement.

The man has his usual grin on his face. "In just a few seconds, that car over there is going to run into that telephone pole."

"I already know there's nothing I can do about it." Mark's shaking voice, lowers in defeat.

"You are right. Do you know who that man is?"

Mark shifts his eyes to meet the man's. "No. Am I supposed to?"

"His name is George. His wife, Ethel, is waiting for him to come home from work. Today was his last day. Tomorrow would be his first day of retirement. He also just celebrated his 50th wedding anniversary."

Mark looks sadly in the direction of the car. It suddenly rams into the pole and bursts into flames. Mark jumps back, nearly tripping over his own shoes. He puts his hands over his mouth to muffle his yelp. In a matter of seconds, there is another small explosion and the entire car is totally engulfed in flames. Unfortunately, the driver never emerges from the hot car.

I have to help him, he thinks to himself.

As if he can read Mark's thoughts, the man reaches out and grabs Mark's arm.

"There's nothing you can do now."

"You don't know that." Mark's eyes begin to fill with tears. As soon as his eyes are maxed out, the tears begin to trickle down his cheek. He can barely see the next chain of events through his clouded vision; even though he has some idea what's going to happen. He thinks about running in the opposite direction; far, far, FAR away from here. Just as the thought crosses his mind, a strong hand reaches out and grabs his forearm again. Mark looks over at the man. He is not looking at Mark but, instead, his gaze is on the accident in front of him.

"Get off me!" He shouts at him over the ruckus of the loud wreck. As the last word leaves his lips, his car comes barreling towards them. Mark tenses up. He watches as it skips onto the sidewalk and narrowly misses striking several pedestrians. However, there is one individual that is unable to get out of harm's way. Mark can hear more screeching and even a loud thud as the body of a full grown man smashes into the front of the car. He flies through the air. Mark watches in horror as the body lands on the sidewalk. Mark sprints toward the body. Unsure if he can make a difference, he kneels down next to the injured man. His eyes are half open and there's a wheezing sound escaping his mouth. Mark tries to comfort the man but even with his hand outstretched, he doesn't feel the body.

Mark doesn't look up. "What was his name?"

"Cameron."

Mark falls backwards and lands in a sitting position. He pulls his knees up to his chest and rests his forehead onto his knees.

"Cameron is a very successful physician. He has a beautiful wife and a young, autistic son named CJ. He lost everything in a house fire accidentally set by CJ. Even through that, he continues to work endlessly to make his son's life the best it can be. Right before you ran him over, he was on his way home to surprise CJ with his favorite cupcake."

He looks up. His other self jumps out of the damaged car. Mark watches as his past self runs into a tiny building. Mark again kneels next to the man on the sidewalk. Before he can check for a pulse, other people run over to help. Mark feels pressure on his arm and he knows who it is. He stands up and walks away from the chaos.

"So, what's the point of all of this?" Mark asks.

"Well, let's come over here and sit down for a minute."

Mark watches the man turn around. He heads right for a nearby picnic table. He sits down and looks over at Mark. He pats the bench next to him. A feeling of defeat washes over Mark and he puts his head down. He drags his feet, kicking pebbles away as he sits down.

"So, how are you feeling?"

Mark angrily snaps his head up. "What do you mean, 'how am I feeling?' I FEEL like you're torturing me. What's the point of showing me this?"

"What do you think is the point of seeing all of this?"

Mark is furious. He leaps to his feet. "Buddy, I don't know…"

Crash.

Mark hits the ground as a sudden loud crash erupts. His chin connects with the concrete. When no other loud sounds follow, he gets to his feet slowly. He spins around to look behind him. Police cars are beginning to line the front of the store. Mark backs away. After only taking a few steps, an outstretched hand stops him.

"Let me go! I don't want to be here."

"Mark."

"I don't know who…"

"Mark."

"What could you possibly…"

"Mark."

Mark stops rambling.

"Come sit down."

Mark walks on a set of shaky legs to the table. He collapses onto the bench. Before he can stop himself, he begins to sob uncontrollably. He buries his head in his hands.

"What have I done?" he wonders miserably.

"Mark."

"What!" he emotionally shouts.

"Mark, it's not about what you've done. It's about what you're going to do now."

Mark picks his head up, confused. Tears stream down his cheek but he makes no attempt to brush them away. He makes eye contact with the man for the first time in several minutes. The man looks back with calm eyes and a gentle smile. He looks over at the building. Although he sees only cops, he knows exactly what is going on inside. "Do you mean, it's not too late to save them?" He springs to his feet and begins running to the deli door.

"Mark."

With only one thought in mind, Mark jumps through the broken door. He pauses to gather his bearings. He sees himself standing against the counter. He doesn't wait to see what happens next, Mark leaps at the gun wielding man. He shuts his eyes tight as he does this.

"Umph."

Mark opens his eyes and sees he has run directly into the counter. The hit both surprises and angers him.

"Mark."

Although it is said very quietly, Mark turns around. He faces the door, expecting to see someone standing there. No one is. Unsure of what to do, Mark walks away from the scene in the deli and reemerges on the sidewalk.

The man is sitting on the bench, calmly waiting.

"What do you want me to do?" Mark spats. "I thought you said I had a chance to fix this."

"Come back and sit down."

"No! I'm tired of listening to your crap. I'm going to fix this."

With no other option, he turns back around. As he nears the door again, he stops in his tracks. A long line of people begin squeezing through the broken door. He steps back to allow them the room to exit. The first to emerge is the injured deli patron. He is being half-carried by another man half his size. Next to follow is a small family and another couple. The look of panic on their faces surprises Mark. When the line finally ends, he watches them scamper away around the wall of cars. He peeks his head inside and sees himself standing behind the counter. He can also see the feet of someone sitting on the floor. Mark climbs into the deli.

"Hey, buddy," he says to himself

No one answers or even acknowledges his entrance.

"Hey, it's Julia, right?" He asks to the girl sitting on the floor. There's no answer from her either. "Can you guys hear me?"

He runs over to himself and begins waving his arms in his face. "Hey, don't do this. Just turn yourself in."

"I bet that's what Julia was hoping he'd do, as well."

Mark turns around and sees the man standing in the doorway amongst the broken glass.

"I don't have time to listen to this again," Mark yells.

"That's just it, you do have the time. Julia is a young, high school student. She helps raise her small niece, has a part time job, goes to high school, and takes care of her alcoholic mother. She makes good grades and is looking forward to going to college. She is going to be the first person in her family to both graduate high school and attend college."

"Oh, Jesus."

"Hello! This is Officer Evans again. We know there are still more people inside. Why don't you let them go and we can talk?"

The real-time Mark begins to panic. He watches as the young girl slowly climbs to her feet. He attempts to stop her but his hands go right through her. He abandons her and returns to himself.

"Stop!" he shouts in desperation. "Please, listen to me."

Nothing he says or does make a difference. He watches in horror as the couple begin their trek to the front door. Mark runs his hands nervously through his hair. He paces in a circle. He can hear the sound of the megaphone but he doesn't pay attention to the words.

"Oh, God!" he finally shouts. "Somebody, please do something!" He looks at his companion. You have to stop them.

The man smiles sadly. "There's nothing we can do. This has already happened."

"Then what's the point of being here again?" Mark panics. "We can't just stand..."

Several gunshots ring out. After a small pause, what seems like an explosion erupts. Mark hits the ground and covers his head. He lies on the ground, sobbing. He hears nothing around him, just the pounding of his heart and his own crying. After several minutes, he lifts his head up. He wipes the drool from his mouth. He looks around, shocked at his surroundings. He leaps to his feet when he realizes he's back at his house.

"How did you do that?" he confusingly shouts.

"Which part?"

Mark spins around and sees the man sitting in the recliner in a relaxed manner.

"How did we get back here? We were just outside. I don't…"

The man holds his hand up. Mark is instantly quiet.

"Instead of answering your question, let me ask you one." Mark is just about to interrupt him with an angry response, but is quieted by a raised hand. "How was your day today?"

"Is this a joke? How do you think my day was?"

"I would prefer if my question wasn't answered with a question. Let's try again. How was your day?"

"My day sucked. Thanks for asking."

"Why was your day so terrible?"

"What the hell, man? What kind of question is that?"

"Why was your day so terrible?"

Mark takes a step toward the man. He balls up his fist even though it is shaking. "Because all those people died."

"Ok. Who killed them?"

"Listen, I don't know who you are or what kind of game you're playing." Mark wipes the snot off his nose on his sleeve.

"Mark, who killed them?"

"You know the answer to that."

"Mark, who killed them?"

Mark releases his fist. He walks over to the couch and throws himself down. He covers his face with his hands. "I did," he says, not above a whisper.

"I'm sorry but I didn't hear you."

"I SAID I DID!" Mark shouts. He's back on his feet. He begins pacing without thinking of what he's doing. He shakes his hands back and forth then wipes his sweaty palms on his jeans.

"Try taking a deep breath."

Mark stops pacing. "Excuse me? After everything you did, you're telling me to take a deep breath?" His face reddens.

"I didn't do anything. Calm down and sit. Let's talk."

"I don't want to talk. I wanted you to help me."

The man is still sitting down. "Please. Sit down."

Mark reluctantly sits down on the couch again. The tears begin to well in his eyes again.

"So..."

"So, what?"

"So, would you like a second chance?"

"What?!"

"Would you like a second chance?"

Mark leaps to his feet. "I can fix this? How?"

"Let me ask you a question."

"No. How can I fix this?"

"Let me ask you a question."

Knowing the man isn't going to give up, he sarcastically responds, "Sure."

"Do you think you've made good choices the last couple of years?"

Mark doesn't initially answer. He's more perplexed by the question. "What kind of question is..." he stops himself. Catching on that only the correct answer will suffice, he changes his answer. "No, probably not. No one's perfect, though."

"You are right. No one is perfect. Everyone makes mistakes. Most of those mistakes don't end up like yours did, do they?"

"Is there really a way I can fix this?"

"There is."

Mark begins pacing again. "What can I do? Do I need to pay for their medical bills? I don't have much money but maybe I can borrow some. Who should I call?"

"That's not what I mean. I'll make you a deal. I will bring back everyone that was hurt today."

"Oh! Yeah, ok! I don't even care how you do it! Thank you!"

"I'm not finished. I'll bring back everyone that was hurt today; except you. You will have to come with me."

"Wait, what? Where would we go?"

"If you would prefer, I can bring you back. You can go back to your mother's house, single, unemployed, angry, and alone. Unfortunately, everyone that was hurt by your irresponsible choices will have to come with me."

"I don't understand where they are going."

"With me. What is your decision?"

Mark looks surprised. "I don't want to die. Are you crazy? It's not my fault those people were in my way. Do I feel bad? Sure. But I'm too young to die."

The man gets to his feet for the first time. "So, is that your decision? I'm giving you the chance to make an unselfish choice. You've spent your entire life making bad choices and never living with the consequences. I'm here to offer you a chance to make this right."

"I don't know what to do."

"Yes, you do." The man walks over to Mark. He places his hand on Mark's shoulder. His eyes are calm and Mark can feel himself relax for the first time since waking up on the floor. "Why don't you take a moment." The man takes several steps back to allow Mark room to think.

Mark forces himself to take several deep breaths. He squeezes his eyes shut tight. His mind plays back to everything he's done and how he felt watching the replay of his actions. The sadness that overwhelmed him when he shot the small children to the ground comes flooding back to him. He tries to shake it off but it lingers. His mind replays that moment when he aims his gun at a small child and he pulled the trigger.

"I am not a kid killer," he mumbles quietly trying to convince himself.

He remembers the desperation he felt when he knew the building was surrounded by police. That moment when he realized there was no way out, was a feeling he didn't want to feel again. He felt anger at himself for allowing drugs, adrenaline, and peer pressure to dictate his decisions. Then his mind jumps to his mother. He's never had a good relationship with her but losing him would crush her. He tries to picture his own funeral and his sobbing mother is the only thing he can envision. Not being able to see his friends, drink another beer, or party with impossibly gorgeous women brings on a new level of sadness. He would have to give up everything he's earned, everything he's ever wanted. Suddenly, the answer becomes clear. He wipes the tears from his eyes and walks straight to the man; with his head up and his shoulders back. With confidence he wasn't aware he possessed, he says, "I've made my decision."

• • •

The sun is shining high in the sky. Although it is still early morning, the heat from the sun is quickly warming up the neighborhood. As usual, the traffic begins to increase as the morning progresses. As usual, the sidewalks are littered with joggers, dog walkers, and bicyclists. One of the bicyclists, Bryan, is busy delivering the morning newspaper. As he nears the next house, he grabs another paper, preparing to throw it. Reaching the driveway, he chucks it toward the unopened garage door. It falls near its intended target. It lands with a *thunk* and falls open. The morning light shines on the headline "Reign of Terror Ends After Suspect is Killed in Police Shoot Out."